Immersion

And Other Tales of Depravity

By
JON CAMPISI

This book is dedicated to all of the creative geniuses who have inspired me throughout the years … and to my loved ones. You know who you are.

Contents

Immersion

I.

Here I sit. Night after night. The blank monitor staring back at me. Laughing at me. It's starting to become routine. I try to focus my attention on something other than the blinking cursor, but of course I can't. And then the bitch comes to mind. Nona has been my literary agent for ten years, and although we've practically been through it all, she told me that if this book isn't finished in three months, I should start looking for a new career. And all I can think of is a time when everything was different. When my books were selling, my marriage was thriving, my son actually wanted to spend time with me. Unfortunately, that seems like a lifetime ago. Nowadays, I pretty much spend my time lounging around what was once a happy home, filled with love and understanding. Somehow along the way though, things changed.

I can't pinpoint the exact time and place, all I know is that things began to take a turn for the worse around the time I was working on my last novel. My wife began telling me that I had a drinking problem, and that I needed to stop, if nothing else then for the kid's sake. I told her there was nothing to worry about; it was a simple case of writer's block. But Judith didn't listen. She never entertained the notion that maybe I was under a lot of pressure and simply needed something to take the edge off. "Toby's having problems in school," she would often say to me during one of these late night quarrels. Of course the exact time of day I was used to getting work done. "You need to put down the bottle and start spending more time with your son." OK, so I had one vice, at least I wasn't a bad husband. A bad father, maybe, but I'm not the one who cheated on her. Of course this only agitated me even further. She just didn't seem to take into consideration that what I was doing, I was doing for the family, to support her and the kid. To my wife, I was some filthy alcoholic who cared about booze and nothing else. Funny, she knew what she was getting into long before she ever said, "I do." I guess now it was different because in her deluded, overprotective mind, our 8 year-old son had some sort of undiagnosed learning disorder like all the other Ritalin children.

I don't lie to myself anymore. I've come to accept the fact that my marriage was probably over long before she slept with that other guy. *At least you're not miserable anymore*, I often tell myself. But who am I kidding. Of course I'm miserable. Now more than ever. I guess it's just a matter of time before I crawl into a hole somewhere to die. But first I should probably try to get some work done. God forbid I keep the bitch waiting another fucking minute. After all, it's only my life we're talking about here. This is just one of many things Nona seemed to have in common with Judith. Both seemed to believe the world centered around her and no one else.

As I sit here, trying to piece my life back together, trying to muster up enough strength to get out of bed let alone finish my book, I can't help but to think that maybe things could have turned out differently. Maybe, I would be a different person today if only I had paid more attention to my family. Well, I suppose it's too late now. They're gone, and I'm here. Alone with nothing but my thoughts and memories, what's left of them anyway. *Yes Nona, you're going to get you're precious manuscript*, I keep telling myself. Really, this is my only true motivation at the present moment. *Don't worry, I'll make you a lot of money, and then I'll go off and crawl into some hole to die.*

This is my life now. This is what fills my days. Who needs these thoughts, these moments of forced regret? Maybe things could have turned out differently, or just maybe, I was destined to be the person I am today, to live the life I have today. Here I sit.

2.

I first met Judith around twelve years ago. Things were different back then. I guess you could call them the innocent times. We didn't worry about things like schools, and house payments. What we did seem to do is spend a lot of our time together in bed. This was the beginning of the relationship, when it seemed as if nothing could go wrong. We didn't have a care or worry in the world.

Toby was what you would call an unplanned pregnancy. My writing career was really beginning to take off, and quite naturally, I was experiencing a sort of natural high. Knowing that I was finally getting some recognition for my work gave me a feeling of indestructibility. Apparently, that wasn't the case in the sack.

"The strip is pink, what the hell does that mean!" Judith screamed from the bathroom. "Beats the shit out of me. Did you try reading the back of the box?" This was the only response I could conjure up at the time. Looking back now, I realize that I probably could have been just a bit more sensitive.

Who did I think I was fooling? I wasn't ready to be a father. And I don't exactly think Judith was ready for the challenges of motherhood either.

"Could you at least get your ass out of bed and come in here and help me!"

I'll never forget that day, that's for sure. And that's also the last time I ever buy one of those home pregnancy tests. The damn doctor is supposed to tell you if you're pregnant, not some piece of recycled plastic.

The arguing soon subsided, and we realized that it was time to face the inevitable; like it or not, we were about to be parents. Everything we strove to avoid at this point in our lives blew up right in front of us.

"So, we'll just have to rethink some things," I told her. But Judith wasn't having any of it. I could tell by the look in her eyes that she saw this as a major blow to our carefully crafted lives as opposed to the positive turning point that it should have been. This isn't to say that Judith wouldn't make a good mom, it's just not what she wanted at this point in her life. So much for mapping out your future.

3.

Toby was born in the beginning of December, right smack dab in the middle of a godforsaken New England winter. Of course our "family" car at the time was a convertible coupe, the perfect vehicle to drive your wife to the hospital in on a twisting, ice-slicked Massachusetts road. Writhing in pain in the small, handcrafted bucket seats in a German made car only a young, childless couple could afford, Judith screamed at the top of her lungs for me to step on the gas. I must admit, thoughts crept into my mind. Evil thoughts. Something was telling me to turn the wheel hard and sharp, putting us both out of our misery. Of course I didn't. I never had the guts to do anything that would require me to take even the slightest amount of initiative. Pulling up to the emergency room, almost passing right by the front entrance thanks to a patch of black ice covered with the white stuff, we were met by a hospital worker who appeared she was getting ready to close up shop. How about that? A hospital closing its doors to the public because of a little snow. I had only hoped as much because it would have given me an excuse to turn right around and visit the "other doctor," the one who would have been able to rid us of this unforeseen problem. In reality, the nurse had just been going outside to catch a smoke.

"We need a wheelchair over here!" he called out to his fellow staffers, waiting in the wings for anything to happen on what was surely one of the slowest days that old place had seen in a long time.

I helped the nurse prop Judith into the chair, almost dropping her when my foot slipped out from under me. Luckily, or unluckily, I guess it depends on how you look at it, I caught myself, and Judith wound up being the only one laid up in the hospital for the next 24 hours.

The snow had in fact gotten so heavy during the birthing process that we were asked by the hospital administrator to stay another day; a rare occurrence in this day and age, what with insurance and all.

****

"It's a boy!" I'll never forget those words. Suddenly, everything I had thought would be a drain on my life got quick turned upside down. It's a hard feeling to describe, holding your very own child in your arms, so small and delicate, no bigger than a loaf of bread.

I'll also never forget the look on Judith's face. I think that was the last time I saw her happy, I mean truly happy. The kind of happy that makes you forget there are wars in the world and starving children. It was as though nothing could ever again bring you down. That soon changed of course, and looking back, the change seemed to have taken place as soon as we set foot back in our home.

4.

Those first few months were awful. There's something about sleep deprivation that makes even the sweetest girl turn cruel. And if the wife's not happy, the husband has no chance whatsoever. Phrases like, "I thought it was your turn to change him," and, "I got up with him last time," became commonplace in our household. Pretty soon, the somewhat organized method of divvying up chores lent itself to a new type of structure; total chaos. It became quite clear that I wasn't going to get any work done anytime soon. And with Judith not working, I had no clue as to where the money would be coming from.

Then came the screaming.

"Can't you understand that I have to be out looking for work! How are we supposed to survive while I'm cranking out the third draft of this thing!"

I had been making quite a name for myself in the writing world at the time, but was having a bit of trouble with my latest project. It was a historical fiction piece on the Black Plague, and I simply didn't have the time or the mindset to jump into this thing full force. Not at this stage in my life. What I needed was some fairly steady freelance work and I wasn't going to find it shacked up with my wife and screaming child in our little fortress in the woods.

That's the other thing. Toby never seemed to shut up. I understand that children cry, that it's a part of their natural development, but something wasn't right. He'd scream his lungs out for no apparent reason for hours on end.

The strange thing was that as he grew older, the verbal complaining never seemed to subside. There must have been something on his little mind, I just had no clue as to what it was.

I think by the time we enrolled him in preschool it became quite apparent that this wasn't your typical 4 year-old child. I mean, he just didn't seem to be happy; *gee, I can only venture a guess where he got that one from.* And of course in my opinion Judith was looking for the answers in all the wrong places, namely in the pages of that awful rag Cosmo and others like it.

Because of our problems at home, I found myself becoming more and more isolated within my own thoughts. My only means of escape was to write, and there was no way I was going to get any of that done in this house.

So I started walking.

It began as a way to sort of take my mind off of things, but soon turned into something more. I started noticing weird things upon my return home from these semi-daily outings. It was almost as though my house was in some sort of different dimension than the rest of the world. I would be hard-pressed to explain exactly what it was I was feeling, except that every time I set foot in my house, a strange feeling overtook me.

I never verbally expressed this to Judith, or anyone else for that matter, but I did begin making regular notations in my journal.

It was also around this same time that Toby exhibited what I can only describe as strange behavior. For instance, he would wake in the middle of the night from a bad dream, yet he never seemed to be too upset. It's as though bad dreams became comforting for him. This I was never able to comprehend.

Granted, I've had my share, especially since I used to pen short horror stories back in my college days – the dreams actually helped me with my writing – but I was simply never able to understand why it was as though he felt right at home with these terrible night visions.

That wasn't all. As he got older, whenever he got into an altercation with a fellow student, he never seemed to be bothered by it. What I mean is that he'd return home with a bloodied lip or scrapes on his knees and elbows, no doubt a common occurrence for any child of that age, but it was almost as though he relished the pain.

Needless to say, this wasn't pleasing my wife.

"Can't you for once teach your son that fighting is not the answer!"

For whatever reason, I always seemed to reply the same way.

"I'll sit down and talk with him soon, hun, just let him rest for the night. He's had a long day."

Judith wasn't having any of it. She was hell-bent on taking him to a shrink, another tip she undoubtedly picked up from one of those supermarket rags, the kind that sit and stare you down at the checkout line.

"For God's sake Judith, don't you think he's just being a kid," I would often tell her.

But I have to admit, the part about him not being phased by any of this creeped me out as well.

5.

As time went by, Judith and I became slightly more
adjusted to the idea of parenthood, yet our own situation
continued to baffle us, me in particular. We began reading
books with awful titles such as "So You're Parents Now"
and "Raising Children" in some half-assed attempt to
educate ourselves on the trials and tribulations of having a
youngster, something neither one of us had any experience
with. In our own families, Judith and I both gained only
child status, and with no respective siblings to look after,
we simply didn't know how to handle things when Toby
arrived.

Nevertheless, we did our best. But our best never seemed to
be good enough. Toby hadn't even finished kindergarten
yet and he was already being threatened with expulsion. I
guess the old expression "keep your hands to yourself"
simply never registered with our son.

He never did get kicked out of school, but I wouldn't exactly say he improved any either. I guess the regular sessions with the school counselor were enough to satisfy the powers that be, that and the constant promises on my part of "handling the situation" at home.

6.

"Ms. Hunsberger will see you now Mr. Lloyd."
I couldn't believe it. His first day of first grade, and he was already getting into scuffles. I just didn't understand; what the hell was there to argue about when your only worry was learning your ABCs.
Elaine Hunsberger must have been the school's principal since it first opened. The woman looked like a great aunt no child would be caught dead kissing on the cheek, let alone basking in her presence. I felt icky just sitting in her office; I could only imagine how the misbehaving youngster felt.

But I also felt annoyed. I was ripped away from my work,
(which these days consisted of covering high school sports
games for the local weekly newspaper – just something to
bring in some cash while I slaved away at my novel), to
stare at this woman's weathered face, and be told how my
son was in dire need of discipline and probably extra love
and affection.

"Have a seat Mr. Lloyd."

"Please, call me Jack. Mr. Lloyd was my father."

"OK, Jack." The way her eyes bugged out when she put
extra emphasis on my first name really got under my skin,
but I tried not to show it.

"Jack, I called you in today because I'm really concerned
about Toby. I was told by Janice Singer – the kindergarten
teacher your son had last year …"

"I know who Mrs. Singer is, I'm not that out of the loop,
contrary to what my wife might have told you."

"Mr. Lloyd – I'm sorry, Jack. I was not trying to imply
anything. I apologize if my tone was a bit condescending.

19

What I was trying to say is that Janice mentioned to me that Toby was having trouble controlling his temper. Now, this is quite a common thing for youngsters his age, especially young boys, but it is something you should attempt to nip in the bud ASAP. That's my professional opinion anyway."

Who did this woman think she was? I'm the father, I know when to discipline my kid. What she had no clue about were the countless hours I spent in his bedroom talking to Toby about fighting, explaining to him how wrong it was. The fact was he just didn't seem to get it. It was almost as if he enjoyed it, like it gave him a sense of purpose. Of course I knew this, but try telling that to the fossil running the ritzy private school Judith insisted on sending our son to.

"Ms. Hunsberger. Thank you for your concern, but I'll handle things from here." Hopefully this time it would be my tone that would send a clear message. "My wife and I are well aware of his difficulty in adjusting to social situations. We're doing the best we can."

"But Mr. Lloyd, I would suggest that you take him to a …"

"I said Judith and I will see to it that our son is taught the error of his ways. Thank you very much for having me in. Good day, madam."

****

During the drive home, it hit me. Maybe Toby was abnormally aggressive and did need to be taken to a children's shrink, if they had such a thing. I'm sure this would please Judith; she was always talking about how these things were best left to the professionals. I told her he was a pain-in-the-ass kid who needed to be disciplined, but Judith didn't believe in spanking. "Children only learn violence through violence," she repeated during what were becoming our regular late night spats.

But as time went by, and things simply weren't looking as though they would improve any, my decision-making process began to become blurred. Although my pride didn't want to allow myself to do so, I eventually caved, and Judith and I sought out a local children's psychiatrist. That

21

decision, although a difficult one for me, was really

cemented after our dog went missing.

7.

Danny Bose was one of my good buddies from college.

Now a well-established reporter for the Boston Globe,

Danny pretty much spent his days on the city streets,

attempting to uncover the latest political scandal or

otherwise attention-grabbing news story. We kept in touch

over the years, but when he landed his dream job and I

decided to settle down, correspondence slowed

significantly.

Up until my recent brush with my own sanity, out-of-the-

blue calls to "Bosey," as we used to call him during the

college days, usually revolved around the Red Sox's or, on

occasion, would take a serious turn, delving into what

seemed to be my good friend's lifetime membership in the bachelorhood club.

"Bosey. It's Jack Lloyd."

"Jesus Christ, man. How the hell you doing?"

"Listen, what's your schedule looking like this week. I'd like to get together – there's been some stuff on my mind I wanted to talk to you about, *off the record*."

We always joked that way, him being a reporter and all. You never knew when he'd be packing his little hidden digital recorder, trying to catch someone off guard. Of course, I never came with any news big enough to land him a Pulitzer. It was just a little friendly banter between the two of us.

"Is everything alright?" Danny always seemed to have this sort of sneaky, almost malicious tone in his voice, as if he were after some big scoop and the recipient was in the dark about it. But I was his friend, not some unnamed source ready to spill his guts with the latest breaking news scandal.

"Look, Bosey. It's about Toby …"

"How the hell is the little bugger? He must be what, 7, 8 years old by now?"

"Six. That's beside the point. He's been acting strange lately. Nothing Judith and I can't handle, of course, but I'd like to talk to you about it. Say, Friday after work? That restaurant we went to the last time I was out there, the one around the corner from your newsroom."

"So family man suburbanite wants to venture into the city for the evening. What *do* I owe the honor?"

"Look, I told you man. This is serious. I'd just rather talk to you in person than over the phone. Besides, it would give me the opportunity to get out of the house for a while. I'm getting cabin fever."

"Alright man, take it easy. I'll meet you at Barnaby's at 6. Sound good?"

"Thanks a lot, man. I'll see you then."

"Hey Lloyd. How's that mutt of yours doing? You know, that little ugly thing you picked up our senior year to impress that chick you were dating'. What's his name, Roger?"

"He's dead Bosey. I'll explain Friday. Goodbye."

As the dial tone would have been reverberating in Danny's ear, he must have been thinking that there was more to this story than the simple family update he had just gotten from his dear old college buddy. And as he would soon find out, there was indeed more. Much more.

8.

"Nona, I need more time. Plain and simple. I've just got too much on my plate right now. The book's gonna have to wait."

The last couple weeks had been a complete blur. Judith finally began looking for work, we were dealing with Toby's temper problem, or whatever you want to call it. The Gazette simply wasn't giving me the hours I needed in

25

order to put food on my table, let alone take our son to see a head doctor. What the hell was the point of a supplemental income?

As for my book project at this point, it was a follow-up to the book about the Black Plague that was published shortly after Toby was born.

Still, it seemed like there was simply no time for in depth writing at this stage of the game.

"Look, Jacky. I understand you're going through a rough time right now, but I've got deadlines to meet. I'm not trying to sound insensitive, but you knew what you were getting into the moment you signed this book deal. And remember, I was able to get you that extension.

"I think what you need is to get away. Go book a weekend in the mountains. I'm sure you could put pen to paper in that solitude."

Was this woman joking? I'm telling her how my family needs me and she's suggesting I go off to a cabin somewhere and leave my wife with our destructive son.

Nona may have been a good agent, but she sure as hell lacked in the caring department.

"I told you. I just can't pick up and leave right now. Judith and Toby need me, and I'm not going to be able to move any quicker on this thing until I get the family situation taken care of."

"I don't know what to tell you kid. If the book's not done soon, we're going to have a serious problem. Try to get some rest, will ya. You're starting to look like the walking dead."

That's my Nona. Always quick with a comforting word.

"I need to get down to the city tomorrow. I'm meeting with an old friend from college. We're going to put back a few and catch up on old times. Is that relaxing enough for you? Maybe I'll take the laptop along and try to get some writing done on the train."

"Jacky, I'm only concerned about you. Yes, I want you to get this book done, but not because I'm a hard-nosed bitch concerned about money and nothing else." *Funny, I thought*

27

she just hit the nail on the head. "You're a good writer

Jack. I know it, you know it, and your fans sure as hell

know it. I'm only pushing you because it seems like you

need a little extra coaxing. Please, get some rest.

Rejuvenate yourself. But then work on churning out some

good copy. I know you've got it in you. Go get 'em tiger."

God, I always hated it when she talked down to me like I

was some helpless 5 year-old who required motivation.

"I'll talk to you later Nona. I've got to go pick Toby up

from school." I paused to look around her office, a room

which clearly contradicted the 'I could care less about

money' speech she gave. "I'll keep you posted."

"Take it easy kid."

9.

It had indeed been quite some time since I had been in the city. It sure was nice to get away, even if it was only for an evening. I did feel bad about leaving Judith alone with our son, who had shown increasing signs of violence in recent time.

I did take my laptop on the train with me, as I had told Nona I would be doing, but the last thing I got done was work. As of late, I had been keeping a journal of sorts, jotting down all those little things I thought were wrong with Toby, including, but not limited to, the restless nights, ever-increasing fits and tantrums, and general unpleasant demeanor. The terrible two's were long over with; something just wasn't right with my son.

Barnaby's was this old tavern situated in downtown Boston. Not only was the building itself marked with a great bit of history, dating all the way back to the early

1800s, but it held a great deal of sentimental value for myself, and others I'm sure. It was the place me and the guys spent a good number of drunken Saturday nights at during college, meeting countless unnamed women and filling our bellies with pitcher after pitcher of Boston's own home brewed lager.

The memory-filled place was even the locale I used to parade Roger outside of, always a good way to impress the ladies.

****

" … say happened to Roger?"

I was getting lost in the memories of this old place again. It always prevented me from keeping my mind focused on the task at hand, whatever that may be at any given moment.

"Jacky boy, I asked you what happened to your dog?"

Bosey and I were sitting where we always sat, at the spot on the bar in between the bathroom and the cash register. That way, if one of us needed to hit the head, a saved seat would be none too far away. It also came in handy when ordering drinks, since a server was always nearby.

"Like I said on the phone, Bosey, Roger's dead. I found him in the woods about a quarter mile from the house. He … he was … (I still found it difficult to talk about, even though the dog had lived a very long life. That dog meant everything to me. I probably loved him more than my wife and kid put together. *Now, now. That type of thinking will get you nowhere.*)

"Roger was stabbed, man. Eighteen times. I took him to the vet, and the guy said Rog had likely been done in by a large kitchen knife." I still couldn't believe it, I mean, who could do such a thing?

"Look man, I'm really sorry, I don't know what to say." Although Bosey didn't have a family of his own, let alone a pet to look after, I still felt comforted in just sharing this with someone. I had told Judith that Rog had been hit by a car, and Toby, well my son never much seemed to care for the little guy. The weird thing was he didn't show the slightest bit of emotion when I told him the old hound had been killed.

"Sometimes kids don't know how to express their feelings, especially when confronted with a difficult situation," Bosey said, knowing full well that he was just delivering a crock of bubbling shit. An overgrown child himself who never grew out of his college days wasn't about to lecture me on the perils of child rearing.

"Look, Jack, not to be the least bit insensitive, but wasn't there another reason why you called me here today? Some urgent matter you wanted to discuss?"

I felt like telling the asshole that finding your dog murdered, dead from multiple stab wounds with no idea as to who committed this crime and why was to me a fucking urgent matter, but I thought the better of myself.

"The thing is," I continued instead, "I'm having problems at home. My son seems to be, what you call, beyond help. Ever since before he was walking, he's been causing trouble. And as he's been growing older, his demeanor has grown increasingly more hostile. He doesn't listen to Judith or I, he constantly gets into fights at school, he can't seem to make friends. I just don't know what to do anymore." My admission in seemingly failed parenting would, under normal circumstances, cause Bosey to make one wisecrack or another about me never being fit to be a father in the first place, but I guess the gravity of the situation caused my old friend to bite his tongue. Instead, he did the next worst thing; he offered another attempt at advice.

"Have you guys taken him to see anybody? A professional I mean?" Bosey was one of those people who no matter if he tried to be serious or not, he just gave off this vibe of goofiness. It just seemed to me as though he thought too much of a real, serious conversation would be detrimental to his aura. I got the impression that what he really wanted to do was slap me on the back, order another round of beers and tell me I'm full of shit. That I was experiencing normal apprehensions and that Toby was your average young boy just coming into his own.

I guess my own demeanor made him think the wiser. "Listen, we tried everything. Discipline at home, (*or as much of it as that bitch wife of mine would allow*), talking with school counselors. I even got an introductory appointment scheduled with the local child shrink. Look, man, I'm just beyond my wits end." Wow, a steaming confession to a guy whose biggest decision probably revolved around whether to order pizza or Chinese.

"But there's more, Bosey," I went on to tell my dear old college friend, the tone of my voice and the look on my face spelling out that there was indeed much more, if I could just bring myself to get it out. Another drink would certainly help. Bosey decided to order us shots of Jameson. I asked for mine to be a double. Nothing like Irish whiskey to help you spill your guts.

I continued: "The day Rog went missing, I found Toby in his room. He wasn't coloring, or watching TV or doing any of the other 'normal' things that kids do. He was just sort of sitting there, staring at the wall. I tried to enlist his help in finding Rog, but he told me that he was just a dog, and that he'd surely find his way back. Funny, but I didn't get the impression that he cared all that much. It wasn't until later that I discovered why, or at least why I think he could have cared less about the situation at hand. Now although I still don't know for sure, and I know it's going to be hard for you to comprehend this, hell, I still have trouble believing it myself, but I have a sneaking suspicion that Toby was somehow involved in Rog's disappearance."

As funny of a guy as Bosey claims to be, he wasn't laughing much now. What he did do was proceed to tell me how just because my son is having behavioral problems, doesn't make him a dog kidnapper, or worse.

"I know how crazy this must sound," I told Bosey, ordering up my third shot of liquid courage, "But it gets worse. I think I found proof that Toby had something to do with … with…" I couldn't even bring myself to utter the words.

"Look, man. When Judith went to make dinner the other day, she had trouble locating a certain favorite knife of

35

hers. It was some sort of heirloom or something, a gaudy piece of shit that has been in her family for generations. Anyway, my curiosity got the best of me, and while Toby was at school a few days later, I searched his room. I eventually found the ugly thing. It was under his bed, wedged in between the mattress and box spring. Bosey, it had dried blood caked on the end of it."

It was at this point that Bosey's I-know-what-you're-going-through comforting look began to disappear. I went on to tell Bosey everything, about how we've had trouble handling Toby ever since he was born and how things seemed to have progressively gotten worse.

We ordered up another pitcher, and, as we drank, things began to become both hazy and clear at the same time.

10.

The next morning, I awoke in Bosey's downtown apartment with the aftertaste of stale ale still lingering on my already filmy morning breath-laden mouth. My insides felt dehydrated and my head ached. In the background were the sounds of a bustling Boston morning, no doubt less intense than would be offered during a weekday. It may have been Saturday, but my entire being called for a massive dose of caffeine as though I were about to head out to the office, that is if I had an office. I sure hoped the ruckus in the other room was my good old friend concocting some of his world famous homebrewed coffee. *If he wasn't, I just may have to sic Toby on his ass. With the way the little demon spawn had been acting lately, I'm sure he would consider it a privilege to off some nosy reporter.* Jesus Christ, I told myself, it's way to early for thoughts like these.

"How ya feelin' in there buddy ol' pal." Well, I guess sunshine in the other room had already risen.

"I could sure use a cup a joe," I called into the kitchen, hoping the response would garner a mug in my hand and not more conversation.

"You sure got loaded last night. Good thing you took the train down. But don't worry, ol' Bosey got you home safe and sound. Oh, and by the way, you may want to call the old ball and chain. She left a message while we were out last night, and you were certainly in no shape to return that call. I think you were passed out before you hit the pillow. *My* pillow, thank you very much."

Bosey had a way of sounding like a dick even when he was clearly joking. It's something I learned to live with while we were in school, (maybe I was just too drunk half the time to care or even notice), but considering the current circumstances, it was beginning to annoy me just a bit. But as always, I turned a smile.

"Yeah, thanks for bringing me back last night. After spilling my guts, I guess I needed to unwind a bit." That and the place. The memories always came flooding back whenever we stopped by that old brick tavern.

The décor in Danny's less-than-expensive apartment could be attributed to both his personality and lifestyle. News clippings, magazines with coffee-stained rings gracing the torn covers and, of course, used paper plates and plastic utensils could be found lining the one-bedroom, third floor dwelling. Yes, the rising journalist and overgrown college student seemed to be right at home in this place.

Of course, I woke up to the lower back pains that could've only been afforded by the virtually nonexistent lumbar support of a 13 year-old sofa bed, but I couldn't complain. At least I wasn't hung-over in a jail cell somewhere after being informed of some havoc I wreaked at the corner bar.

"So what did Judith say?" I said in a whispered voice, nodding in appreciation at the steaming cup of coffee I was being handed. "Was she pissed?"

"Oh yeah," Bosey replied, of course accompanied by that ever-present shit-eatin' grin. "I wouldn't go home at this point if I were you."

"Yeah, well Judith will get over it. First things first. Got any Excedrin?"

I used to live on the stuff during school, especially if we got tuned up the night before a big exam, something that seemed to happen more often than not.

"Listen, Jack. I know we were both a little lit last night, so I'm gonna' give you the benefit of the doubt." But before Danny got the words out, I already knew what he was going to say. He would undoubtedly tell me that accusing my little 5 year-old boy, who probably only suffered some mild behavior disorder, of kidnapping and murder was a little over the top, scratch that, *a lot* over the top. He would go on to say that the writer's block was beginning to get the best of me and that it was all in my head. There was surely an explanation for what happened to my 13 year-old

Cocker Spaniel other than my bi-polar son taking a knife in his little hands and draining the mutt's life force.

"I know what you're thinking Bosey. But you're wrong. I'm not overreacting. If you lived with us, if you saw what Judith and I see day in and day out, it wouldn't seem that far fetched to think that Toby had something to do with this. And no, the bloodied knife was not part of some school science experiment or a Halloween prop. He's five for Christ's sake!"

I had to get a hold of myself. This whole thing was driving me crazy. And Danny was surely just here to help. No need to take things out on him.

"Look, Jack. All's I'm saying is that maybe things just aren't as they appear. It might do you good to talk to someone about this."

Isn't that what I called you up for asshole!

"I know, Bosey. I know. This whole thing's just got me so crazy."

41

But the truth was I didn't know shit. I had no idea how to tell Judith about this, let alone confront our son. I didn't know who I was supposed to spill my guts to – certainly not the police. Things seemed like they went full circle. As always, bachelor Danny was good for nothing except a few drinks and some laughs. I know he only means well, but I wasn't about to get solid advice from a slightly graying overgrown frat boy now was I? What the hell was I thinking?

Then I decided to phone Judith back. Things had only begun to get bad.

II.

By the time I hung up the phone with Judith, my headache had returned. Of course, she decided to launch into this rant about me being irresponsible and acting like some college kid when I up and left for an evening with Bosey. Funny, but I thought a night away might help me with my sanity, and in turn, help me deal with my family in a rational way. After multiple cups of coffee, a second dose of Excedrin, and a nice hot shower, I thanked my old pal for his hospitality and headed home. I couldn't bear the excitement of what I was about to encounter upon my return.

****

"Thank God. Do you know what *your* son has been up to while you were out gallivanting?"

Nice to see you too Judith, darling, light of my life.

"Just calm down and tell me what happened."

"Well, where do I begin. I told Toby I was going to take a shower, and that he should just sit still and watch his cartoons. What do I discover when I get out? He decided to take out his markers and draw all over the living room walls."

I tried to console her, but no matter what I seemed to say, nothing was helping the situation any.

"All right, where is he, I'll talk to him."

43

"Actually, there's more. What he drew, that's really what shocked me. I don't think there's any way to describe it. You have to see it for yourself."

As my wife accompanied me into the living room, I saw something no father should ever have to see. There, before my eyes, in red and black marker, was what I could only imagine as being a depiction of Roger's death: an elementary, stick-figure drawing of a dog meeting his demise with a long kitchen blade. What happened next was something I wished to forget.

"Where's the little fucker, we've got some talking to do."

"Jack, listen, you don't know what that drawing means. It may not mean anything at all. Drawing violent pictures doesn't necessarily mean that a child is ..."

"Look, Judith. There's something I haven't told you about the day I found Roger. He wasn't hit by a car, alright. He was stabbed. Many, many times."

"Jack Lloyd, don't you dare tell me that because of this drawing, you think our son ..."

"What I'm telling you, Judith, is that it's about time I had a little chat with our son. He has to be taught right from wrong. And by the way, that knife you were looking for, I found it. The thing was in Toby's room. What's worse is it had dried blood on it."

And with that, it was off to our son's room. It was time for our little angel to find out that dad was no pushover.

12.

Well, I guess I don't have to spell out what happened next. I officially crossed the line; I hit my son. But I didn't just slap him and tell him that drawing on the walls was wrong, I really laid into him. Gave him a good wallop. The worst part about it though was that after I confronted him about the Roger situation, and he refused to admit what I know in my heart he did, I became even more enraged. By the time I was done with him, a decision had been made. Judith wanted me out and I guess I couldn't blame her. It was time I got out of that house anyway. I thought if I would spend another minute there, someone else was going to get hurt. So I grabbed some essentials and out the door I went.

****

"Bosey, it's me, Jack."

"Well, what do I owe the pleasure this time around?"

"Look, I'm sorry to have to do this to you, but you think I could stay with you? Just for a couple of days, until things calm down around here."

I really didn't have anywhere else to go; I was hoping my old pal would take me in. But I wasn't one to beg.

"What the hell happened?"

"After our last little visit, Judith accused me of running away from our problems. I told her I was just in need of a little me-time, but she thought it was about her."

Of course, it was just like Judith to think of herself and no one else.

"How long did you have in mind, I mean staying here."

"Just a couple days, I promise. Just until I get back on my feet."

In reality, I had no idea how I was going to make it up to Judith. I knew I lost my cool, but at this point, I had no idea how I was going to make things right again. The worst part about it was that I really didn't feel all that bad about what I did to Toby. I actually felt relieved after I struck him. It was almost as if it was out of my control. To Judith, I had reached a new low, but in my mind, things were becoming clearer. There was something evil dwelling inside our son and it needed to be shown the light. I had a duty to do, and nothing, especially not some bitch wife, was going to stop me.

But staying with Bosey would turn out not to be the smartest move in the world. And that's when the drinking took a turn for the worse.

47

13.

Staying with my old college buddy had its ups and downs. Sure, for the first couple of days it was like we were kids again; going out partying every night, no wife and son to have to come home to. But I realized that a good thing can only last so long. I guess deep down, I knew I had a responsibility to my family, but it just didn't seem to register. I suppose it was stubbornness that got me in the end.

"You're drunk again, aren't you." If the sound of Judith's voice irked me when I was sober, hearing it when I was under the influence made it damn near intolerable.

"Look, Bosey's been kind enough to let me stay here with him. The least I could do was go out and donate a couple of six packs to the cause."

"Did he even get a chance to have any? It sounds like you're taking pretty good care of things in the booze department."

It's a wonder I was ever able to live with this woman in the first place. Was she always such a nag? I felt like telling her that the reason I was out of the house, the reason I was drinking so heavily again, was her and our demon spawn. But of course I didn't. It would have only aggravated the situation. What I did do was tell her that I was taking some time for myself, and that as soon as I had things worked out in my head, I'd be coming home.

"Look, hun, I'm really sorry about hitting Toby. I promise, I won't do it again. Just let me get this out of my system and I'll be able to come home."

"Jack, how can I forgive such a thing. You know how my father treated us. I always promised myself that if I ever ended up with a man like him, I'd get out, and get out quick."

"I know. And I don't know what else to say. I'm a good father, Judith. But the fact remains; we need to seriously sit down and talk about our son. There's something not right with him."

"He just has some discipline issues, Jack, what he needs is ..."

"It's more than that hun, and you know it."

"Just stop it Jack, all right? I don't want to hear any more about your ridiculous fantasies. I think you're the one who needs help."

"Hun, I know it sounds crazy, but seeing as how strange Toby's been acting lately, I don't see how you couldn't even entertain the possibility that ..."

"Entertain what possibility? That our son is some kind of killer, some kind of wicked demon?"

And although Judith was obviously being sarcastic, my obligatory 'that's exactly what I'm saying response' did nothing to calm her down any.

"Can't you see that something hasn't been right with our son since day one," I told my wife, serious as can be. "You know he's had behavioral difficulties, trouble adjusting to social settings. Christ hun, all the signs are there."

"What signs?" Judith responded. "You think our son is some sort of psychopath?"

"I don't think Toby is a psychopath, dear."

Judith sounded relieved, if only for a second. "Thank God, I thought you were gonna say ..."

"I believe he's possessed."

Judith's frustration mounted, and she laid into me.

"How could you say such a thing! We haven't even taken him to be seriously analyzed. Jesus, talk about jumping to conclusions."

And with that, Judith had said her piece.

"Jack Lloyd, I don't think I know you anymore. You know what I think? I think you need to stop drinking and get some help. Call me when you're better."

Then she hung up and I was left with the lingering thought that I wouldn't be seeing my wife or son for quite some time. But another thought crept into my head ... Judith was left alone with Toby, and I just didn't feel that was the best situation, for either one of them.

14.

Bosey gave me the OK to stay with him indefinitely. I suppose he was all about helping out a friend in need. Either that or he wanted the rights to the book when all was said and done. I guess my life just had the makings of a great story. And the crazier and more dramatic it became, the better for sales.

****

As the weeks went by, I couldn't help but to think I left my family all alone to fend for themselves. But what was I to do? Judith wanted me out, at least until I got off the booze.

Our son, well, God only knows what he was up to. I wanted to help, I really did. But I couldn't go back there. Not like this. I mean, I cared about my family and all, but I just didn't have it in me. Not what I needed to do to ensure that everything would be all right. No. What I needed was someone who had experience in these sorts of things. I needed someone who knew how to handle evil, the sort of evil we were taught about as children. I needed a religious man. But where was I to start? I was never particularly religious, and Judith was always a nonbeliever. No. The more I thought about it, I came to the conclusion that I was going to have to handle things myself. So I decided to go back home. I thanked Bosey for the moral support, but told him it was time to get back to my responsibilities. No more messing around like when we were kids. It was time to go home. But before I did, one last drink was in order. So we went out and did just that.

15.

When I got back to the house, it seemed as though nothing at all had changed. I don't know what I was expecting. Being a writer and all, I guess I had already envisioned the ending the way I wanted to see it, but that just wasn't going to happen. No. I had to take matters into my own hands; it was time this father got his family back in order. The way it should be. So upon entering the house, I sat Judith and Toby down. And that's when things got out of control. I guess I shouldn't have reached for the bottle I had brought back with me from Bosey's. But I did. And let me tell you, I have lived to regret it.

"No, you listen to me. I won't have this family deteriorate any more than it already has," I told Judith, Toby sitting in earshot next to her. "Things are falling apart, and we have to do something about it."

"What do you expect me to do," Judith shot back. "Our son is obviously sick and needs help. But you. You're out gallivanting with old chums, reliving old college days. Face it Jack, you're not around because you don't want to be. You don't care about us, Jack, no matter what type of show you put on."

And that's when it happened. I didn't realize it until after the fact, but the bottle I had so willingly accepted from Bosey as a parting gift somehow landed on the side of Judith's head. Sure there were screams, but it was the silence that scared me. The screams came from our son, who was huddled on the floor next to his mother. The silence was Judith; she was passed out on the ground with a streak of blood running from her left temple onto the linoleum floor. As I crept up closer to inspect, it was Toby who attempted to back me away using only his little fist and what he envisioned as strong words.

"You stay away from us," he said, his little voice a mixture of trepidation and naiveté. "You hurt mommy. That wasn't nice."

Well, you hurt my dog, who meant more to me than you ever could, and he's never coming back, I thought. But of course I kept these things to myself. I wasn't going to cure our son with harsh words alone.

"Listen Toby. Mommy just needed a little discipline. You'll understand someday," I told the demon spawn, knowing full well that he had no idea what I was talking about, and also that he would never make it to adulthood. But I do imagine he had some idea of what was going on.

"Toby, now that mommy's out of the way, there's something we need to talk about."

I couldn't believe I was talking this way myself, but it had to be done. I needed to get my son alone, and the opportunity had finally presented itself.

"Son, I need you to tell me the truth about Rog. He didn't really get lost in the woods, did he."

There was a blank look on Toby's face. The look that said, 'Daddy, I have no idea what you're talking about,' but in actuality presented guilt.

I still had my overnight bag in my right hand, and decided it was time to start threatening. If I wasn't going to get straight answers out of my son through mere communication, it was time to convince him otherwise. So I pulled out the pocketknife; the same one I used to pick the new lock Judith had installed on the front door while I was staying at Bosey's. (OK, so I wasn't exactly welcomed home with welcome arms. I guess I left that part out.) But just when I was about to start getting some answers from my son, I felt a sharp pain against the back of my head. I later found out that it was a frying pan, but at the time I just saw darkness. Women. You just can't trust them, can you?

16.

When I came to, I was sitting in our basement, my hands
tied behind my back. The dim lighting resonated through
the narrow staircase leading down to where I was being
held captive. Can you believe that? I was being held a
prisoner in my own home. Go figure. And all I wanted to
do was cure my son; make my wife see the light. But as I
said earlier, Judith never cared about anyone but herself.
Sure, deep down she loved our son, I guess. But then why
wouldn't she listen to me about his condition? I was the
one looking out for him. She was just in denial.

"Get down here and untie me from this chair you bitch."

I guess Judith was out of earshot. Either that or she was
ignoring me. Wouldn't that be a shock. My loving, caring
wife. Ignoring me. I could never have imagined that
happening.

"Look, Judith, I'm sorry I hit you. It won't happen again, OK. I guess I just let my emotions get the best of me. You know how it is. You're a woman for Christ's sake!" I guess playing the gender card wasn't helping my cause.

"Goddamn it, Jack. I told you, after my childhood, I would never stand for a man laying his hands on me. And especially not on my child. Well, now you're going to pay, and pay good.

That's when I heard the footsteps coming down the creaky old stairs in our log cabin-like home in the woods. A home once filled with love and understanding. Goals and dreams. Now it had denigrated to a home of payback, and I was being held in what was to become the basement of pain. The type of pain I couldn't imagine. Not the type I was ready to inflict on my possessed son, and certainly not the type I was prepared to use against my wife, even if she was delusional.

"Hey baby, how you feeling?"

"Judith, please. Untie me. I never meant to hurt you. I just lost my cool was all."

But Judith wasn't having any of it. She wanted retribution. But the funny thing was, I felt like she was taking years worth of both emotional pain and physical abuse out on me. This wasn't about me hitting her, for the first and only time in our entire marriage, mind you, or me threatening our son. No. This was something that ran deep. So deep, in fact, that there was simply no turning back. So she burned me, and burned me good.

"How does it feel, Jacky boy. How does it feel to have the one you love, or thought loved you, turn on you?"

The pain was in fact so bad that for a second, I felt as though I might loose consciousness. But I stuck it out. There was no way she was going to have the satisfaction.

I don't know if it was the eventual numbness from the red hot fireplace poker against my abdomen, or the emotional toll that had been building up, but I decided right then and there not to give up. Obviously, Toby wasn't the only one who had issues. I suppose there was no getting around the fact that there were some crazy genes running in Judith's family.

And although my mind was still in it, I guess there does come a point when the body can only take so much. When the torturous fireplace poker game reached my groin, I started seeing stars. But the weird thing was, I also started hearing things. I could have sworn I heard Roger's bark, but of course that was impossible. Rog was dead, and I wasn't going to solve his death sitting here with my crazy bitch wife playing a little game of 'avenge my childhood abuse using my husband as a stand-in.'

So as I began to fade away and lose consciousness, even though I told myself I wouldn't. And I couldn't help but to continue hearing the sounds of my deceased dog. It's funny, but when confronted with a traumatic experience, the human mind will conjure up things it never thought possible; like the sounds of an old friend. Imagine my surprise when I discovered those sounds were as real as you and I.

17.

As I came to, all I heard was screaming. But this time, it wasn't me, or my son. It was Judith. And the site was enough to make me recoil in horror. There stood Roger, as plain as day. I couldn't believe it. He had returned. I don't know how he did it, but here he was, in the flesh. The pain looked unbearable; the hand in which Judith held the red hot fireplace poker now lying detached on the damp, basement floor. Rog's facial mane was matted in blood; blood from his former owner. OK, co-owner. Judith never really liked Roger anyway. She was never a dog person. It was my dog from my college days, and it was I who always took care of him. Judith never really gave a damn, and now it came back to bite her in the ass, or in the hand, as it was. "Get this Goddamn thing off of me!" Judith shouted, her voice echoing in the basement. Meanwhile, Toby had been hiding out in his room, or at least I surmised. I pictured him camping out under his bed, like all frightened children do in a moment of shock and disbelief.

Judith was swatting at Rog with her good arm, but to no avail. He had her right arm in his grip pretty effectively and the blood loss alone was beginning to take its toll.

"Rog, let go boy." I pleaded with what could only be an apparition. But it wasn't. It was my best friend, and he had returned to save my life.

"Please, boy, let go of Judith." And he did. But only for a brief moment. As I turned to see what was happening, I quickly realized that Judith had somehow gotten her other hand back on the fireplace poker, and in that instance, it had ended as fast as it had begun. The dog who had returned back to life leaped toward Judith and got her good, clamping down on her jugular and ending what I never really thought was a good marriage anyway.

It was then that I realized that the wet, misty sensation wasn't a leak in the ceiling, but the blood spewing from Judith's neck. And then she went limp. And once again, I passed out. And the next time I awoke, Roger was by my side, and it was my son that I was facing.

18.

So there he was, in all his glory. My little boy. Staring at me with that lifeless look in his eyes I had become so accustomed to seeing as of late. But he wasn't alone as it were. In his little, albeit claw like hands, were the pair of scissors with which I would often use to cut his hair. For a fleeting moment, memories came drifting by. Judith and I moving up to our little cabin in the woods. Toby's birth. All the good things that I seemed to have forgotten. And then the other memories were drudged up. Toby in school causing all kinds of problems. Judith and I fighting over God knows what. Me and my relapse with the bottle. It all came back to me as I looked my son squarely in the eyes, or what should have been a young boy's eyes. Instead, all I saw was evil. The evil that Judith could never see, and now would never see. I knew something was wrong from the time when he started getting into fights at school, but Judith would never listen. Well, I guess there's no use dwelling on the past at this point. Judith was lying lifeless on the ground, I was tied up in a chair and the demon spawn was eyeing me up as if he was preparing to rid the world of me, Jack Lloyd, the person who gave him life. I decided right then and there that I wasn't about to let this little shit do me in like this. Hell no. There was no way this little crazy bastard was getting rid of me that easy. So I pleaded with him.

"Toby, put the scissors down," I said in a calm, and loving voice. "You're not going to solve anything with them." His response, however, told me that he had no plans on retreating at this point.

"You hurt mommy, and now I'm going to hurt you back."
It was strange, but it was almost like his voice didn't
belong to him at all. It sounded older, more diabolical.
"Now listen, son. Mommy had an accident. It wasn't
anybody's fault."
But Toby clearly wasn't buying it. The problem for him
was that Rog was still by my side, and wasn't going
anywhere until I was freed. So that's when, without being
told, he jumped into action. Somehow, this smart mutt
knew to bite off my knots at that particular moment. If he
didn't, well, I just don't want to think about what might
have happened. Once I was free from the restraints, I leapt
toward my son, knocking the scissors out of his little, yet
strong, hands. I cradled him in my arms and told him
everything was going to be alright. But there was never a
tear shed on his part. Somehow I knew it had something to
do with the fact that he was not totally human. So I
proceeded to do what I never thought imaginable. I was
going to sacrifice my son.

19.

Clearly, this was the only solution. I always knew

something was wrong with my son. Very wrong. But

nobody would listen. Not Judith, not Toby's teacher. No. I,

Jack Lloyd, was the only one who really understood what

was going on here. Our son was clearly possessed by some

supernatural force, and I was going to eliminate him from

this world. It's funny, but before this whole ordeal, I was

never much of a religious man. I mean, ten years ago, if

you would have told me I was going to go on to have a

child who would be controlled by evil forces, I would have

told you that you were the one with problems. But not now.

Now I can see clearly, without any distractions. Toby

wasn't right, he was ill. Seriously ill. And I wasn't about to

let him go on and contaminate the rest of us. So I came up

with a solution.

After Rog set me free from the confines of the chair, I was able to subdue Toby. I made sure he had no other weapons on him, and then took him outback. Living in the woods had its advantages; nobody was around to hassle you about making noise.

I took my son, (although I hesitated to call him that at this point), over to the pit where we used to roast hotdogs in summers past. Once again, the fond memories started to flow. *No, no. Block them out. You know what you have to do, for yourself, and for all of humanity.* I proceeded to tie Toby up, and placed him on the rock shelf lining the pit. "Daddy, please. I'll be a good boy. I didn't really want to hurt you. I only wanted to cut you loose from the chair." And he expected me to believe that he was going to free me from the ropes down in that dingy basement. No. I knew what he was really up to. It's just a shame that he didn't know what he was. The more I thought about it, I kind of felt sorry for the kid. He didn't know what was wrong with him. I did, and that made me both insightful and cursed at the same time. Cursed because I knew what I had to do, even thought it wasn't going to be pretty. But I had to do it. And now, there wasn't a nonbelieving bitch wife to stop me.

"Daddy, please stop."

But his words weren't enough to prevent me from ridding the world of this awful evil. I was dead set on what I was about to do, and nothing was going to stop me. I had the power. I was God at this moment, and I was charged with the most important thing anyone has had to do in quite some time. Maybe more. So, without hesitation, I lit the match. And as the red hot flames began to burn, and the shrieking and screaming echoed in the woods, I was praising the good lord above for instilling me with the courage for doing what I knew had to be done. After all, if I let this evil run amuck in this world, I would be to blame, and Jack Lloyd wasn't a sucker. No thank you. I was strong-willed and I wasn't about to let anyone stop me from fulfilling my destiny.

****

By the time I got the fire extinguisher, and put out all the

flames, there was nothing left of my son but ashes and dust.

Funny, but shouldn't the bones still be intact? Oh well, I

guess minor details weren't a concern at this point. The

important thing was that the evil was gone. There was

nothing Toby could do to anyone at this point. He was gone

and I was left standing. The way it should be. So I took

Rog, and we went inside the house for a nap. It was the first

real sleep I had gotten in months. And it felt good. That is,

until I was awoken.

20.

"Hello. Jacky boy, are you up?"

The knocking on the door just wouldn't subside. "Hello?

Hello?"

"Leave me be. It's been a long day." Well, I thought I was

having a good nap, that was until this shit started up.

I didn't care who was at the Goddamn door. I needed sleep, and sleep was where I turned my attention back to. So I turned back around on the couch and slipped back into dreamland.

When I came to, I heard the sound of paper rustling in the other room. So I carefully got up off of the sofa, grabbed a letter opener that was on my coffee table, and ventured into the kitchen, which is where the noise was originating from.

"Don't think about moving, I have a gun," I announced, only to be met with laughter.

"Jesus, Jack, if ever there was a time I pictured you maiming me with a weapon, it sure wouldn't be when I was in your home. I'd envision it happening in my office, after I told you that you were finished. That you had nothing left in you."

I knew that voice anywhere, it was Nona, my bitch literary agent. But how the hell did she get in?

"You're probably wondering how I got in, right?"

Jesus, was she always this intuitive?

"The key under your welcome mat, silly. Did you forget I knew it was there?"

Nona. What a sight for sore eyes. We may have had our problems in the past, but little did she know that I needed someone to talk to, and fast.

"Listen, Nona, there's something I need to tell you."

"Hey, before you go getting all sappy on me, just know that I was never prepared to give up on you. I always knew you had it in you, Jacky boy. You're a damn good writer. You just needed a little motivation. Well, you sure seemed to have found it. I don't know where, but it sure shows. This is good shit."

She was waving what appeared to be a manuscript around in the air.

"Nona, what the hell are you talking about? You know I've had writer's block for God knows how long now."

"You call this writer's block?" she said, once again waving the stack of papers around. "This is good shit. I guess I now know what you've been up to all this time, shacked up here alone in the woods."

Alone. How the hell did she know I was alone? I wasn't asleep for that long, was I?

I was starting to become worried at this point. Did word get out that I was alone, that Judith and Toby were missing?

"Hey, Nona. How did you know I was alone up here," I asked her. "I mean, was there something on the news?"

Jesus, how long had I been asleep?

"What the fuck are you talking about, Jacky? You've been alone up here for months working on your book. Or at least that's what you told me you were doing. Should I be worried?"

It's funny, but the tone of Nona's voice brought everything back into the here and now.

"Nona, I just wanted to say that despite how I felt about you before ... "

"Jacky boy, how you felt about me before is irrelevant. This is award-winning shit, and don't think I haven't noticed."

OK, so I was officially confused.

"Listen, Nona. There's something I need to tell you."

But she stopped me before I could continue. "Jacky, I know you've been having a difficult time and all. Trying to come up with a book we could actually sell. But let me just tell you, what I have here in front of my eyes. This is good shit."

I had no idea what the hell she was talking about.

"Nona, I'm sorry I haven't been focusing my attention on my writing, but if you would just listen to me for one minute ..."

"Haven't been focusing on your writing? Did you not hear what I just said? This is phenomenal. A bitch for a wife, the anti-Christ for a son, a dog who wouldn't die. It's practically the fucking trifecta of novel writing.

And it was in that moment that my world began to fall apart.

"Nona, I don't think you understand ..."

"Oh, I understand alright. All you wanted was some time alone, and let me tell you, it worked. Listen to me Jacky. This is probably some of the best work you have churned out in years. And I'm not just saying that. I mean it. It's really good."

I didn't understand what was going on. How did she know about Judith and Toby? Had I kept a journal or something?

"Jacky. Let me just say that this is going to go over very good. Very fucking good. The whole crazy husband/father thing. It's in, man. Jacky, this is going to solve all your financial problems."

I was a lost man. I couldn't believe what was happening to me. Was I hearing things right? Was there never a Judith? A Toby? That my overworked, deluded mind created them? I didn't know what to do. I felt lost, sick and utterly alone.

"Jacky, what's the matter? Your problems are solved. I'm telling you, I'm going to sell this manuscript, and you're going to be without a care or worry in the world. This is your lucky break, Jacky. You have nothing to worry about."

But Nona had something to worry about. She obviously didn't know what was going on here. I was trying to explain to her what had happened. But she didn't want to listen. She seemed to think that what I wrote about Judith and Toby was made up fiction. But I knew the truth. So I took matters into my own hands.

"Jack, what are you doing! Let go of me!"

Judith, *I mean Nona*, just didn't understand. If she wasn't going to help, she was only a liability.

"Jack, for Christ's sake! What the hell's the matter with you?! Have you gone nuts?! Let me go!"

Good ol' Nona, she just didn't know when to let up.

"My God, Jacky, all I want to do is help you. Why are you doing this?!"

But, there was no turning back. Not at this point. Nona just didn't understand. She was the only witness to what had occurred between myself and my family. *My family. How 'bout that?*

"Jack, you've gone fucking crazy! Let me go!"

But of course, I couldn't. I knew what I had to do. It was time to put this whole thing to bed. And so I took Nona out to the fire pit. The final resting place of my demon spawn of a son. And I told her whom she'd be joining.

"I don't know what the hell you're talking about! You never had a Goddamn son, Jack! You've been a single man as long as I've known you, now let me go!"

I guess Judith, *I mean Nona*, just didn't understand. It was time to join Toby, and there was no turning back. It was then that I turned around to see Rog staring at me with that awkward glance. It's funny, but as much as I was starting to see what Nona was telling me, I just wasn't ready to believe it. I was Jacky Lloyd.

Hardworking husband and father. Savior of all that is

good and holy. It was my duty to cleanse the world of

that which was evil and wrong. I wasn't about to let

some delusional literary agent tell me what I had to do. I

knew what I had to do.

"Jack, why are you doing this! That was the best work

you've ever done. Don't do this to me!"

And at that moment, I heard my son's voice. He was

calling to me from beyond. Telling me to do what I knew

had to be done. And so I did. And the screams from the

fire pit will be forever etched in my mind.

"Let me go, Jack. Let me go!"

But of course I couldn't. Judith, *I mean Nona*, needed to

be eliminated from this world. And I was the one who

had been chosen to do the deed. Because I was Jack

Lloyd. Cleanser of all that was unholy. And she was

Nona. She was the evil represented in this world. And

no matter how hard I wanted to stop the match from

striking in my hand, I just couldn't do it. And so the red-hot flames burst forth, and the screams echoed throughout the empty woods, and all I was left with were my thoughts. The thoughts of what were once my life, or at least what I thought was my life. And so I proceeded to finish the task with a steady hand.

****

And so now, here I sit. With nothing but my thoughts and memories. Where am I going, where have I been? This is my life now. This is what fills my days. Who needs these thoughts, these moments of forced regret. Maybe things could have turned out differently. Or maybe, just maybe, I was destined to be the person I am today. To live the life I have today. Here I sit.

The Craving

The stranger walked into the bar and ordered up the only
thing he ever drank: plain tonic water with lemon.

His accent said he was from out of town. He also came
across as somewhat old-fashioned, summoning the waitress
with "ma'am," and "darlin'."

Everything about him said friendly, calm, polite. In fact,
there didn't seem to be anything out of the ordinary
concerning this man from another place.

Until, that is, he pulled out a 12-inch Bowie knife and
stabbed a fellow patron in the back.

******

Tim Mulroney was working on his favorite car that
morning, a 1974 Chevy Camaro. He always worked on the
beast when he was feeling stress in his life, or when the
weight of the world seemed too much to bear.

It had been a rough couple years. The death of his son, the
subsequent demise of his marriage. At first, Mulroney took
to drinking – heavily. But when he got that DUI, he wised
up, realizing he got off easy: he could have killed someone,

but he didn't. Realizing it would be unforgivable to cause someone else the pain of losing a child that he himself had experienced, Tim up and quit drinking cold turkey.

It was difficult at first, but he got through it. Nowadays, the only thing that seemed to give him pleasure was working on that sweet vehicle of his.

That's what he was doing the evening that the stranger on a Harley went cruising by Tim's lakefront property.

******

The last thing Doris wanted to do that night was cover a shift for a younger, more able-bodied barkeep. But she did. Doris was the nice one, the one who couldn't say no. Sure, she was 60 years old, beaten down, tired, jaded. All in all, it had been a rough six decades, and the only thing Doris wanted to do was sit back and relax. But with her husband out of work, her medical bills piling up, a sick mother she had to take in and care for, and health insurance to pay for, (since the bar was not about to start offering benefits), Doris simply couldn't turn down the hours.

When the sounds of the Harley roaring down the street made its way to the parking lot of the sleepy, lakeside bar, and the soothing demeanor of its operator soon taking over the small, family-run establishment, Doris felt a surge of hope for once in her life. Hope that this night would be different. Perhaps something could distract her from the typical catcalls of the local drunks, who would think nothing to ask Doris to remove her top, or perform one unspeakable act or another.

Doris, who was used to feeling shitty, used and unappreciated, was hoping this night would be different. She just didn't know how different it would be.

******

Booze made Johnny Bowers feel invincible. He knew in his heart he shouldn't drink, what with alcoholism running in his family and all. But he just couldn't help himself. After a long day on the construction site the only thing Johnny, 35 and single, wanted to do was knock back a few cold ones. The problem is that a few often turned into a slew.

85

When he got to the bar that night Johnny was already

pissed off. His boss had been riding him all day. His

foreclosure notice told of a future living in either a motel

room, or a cardboard box. His body hurt from manual

labor, and he kept thinking if he felt this way now, in his

mid-thirties, what the hell would he feel like in 10 years, or

20.

It was an overall bad day, and all Johnny wanted to do was

feel the warm rush of alcohol running down his gullet. So,

needless to say, when he arrived at the local watering hole

to learn his favorite beer had already been tapped, a sour

mood turned even sourer.

"Jesus Christ on a cracker, Doris," Johnny yelled to the

already miserable barmaid. "Are you shittin' me?"

"Sorry Johnny. Out of my control."

Doris was no pushover. She knew how to handle herself

among the likes of Johnny Bowers. After all, if the beatings

she took from her daddy as a little girl weren't enough to

keep her down, nothing would break this tough old broad.

"Just order something else, would ya?"

It was around this time that the rumbling sounds of a Harley muffler were heard rolling up the dirt road leading to Micky's, a small corner bar that had served the quiet lake community for decades.

In walked a man whose only aim, at first, at least, was to wrap his hands around a cold drink, the more ice, the better. Doris was immediately struck by the stranger's tone; calm, quiet, yet assertive.

The withered bartender dispatched the man's order. As the spur-heeled stranger accepted the cold glass, he held it for a moment, seemingly praying over its contents. Then he drank it back.

"Another please, miss," was the man's only words for the next few minutes.

As Doris went to retrieve the man's second order, she was stopped in her tracks by the blood-curdling screams of another customer. She turned to see the knife protruding from the patron's back, blood running down the chrome bar stool and onto the linoleum floor.

******

It's funny, but while Tim Mulroney had been doing really good with the whole non-drinking thing lately, there was something about the sound of that motorcycle passing by his home that got the young man thinking. What if he would just stop by Micky's for *one* drink, just one, and then be on his way? He should have enough will power to tell himself one, and no more. He'd just stop by, say hi to his old compatriots, knock back a single beer, and be on his way.

Against his better judgment, Tim Mulroney decided to go with his gut. So he put down the tools, pulled the tarp over the Camaro, hopped on his bicycle, (he wasn't chancing another DUI), and set off for his old favorite corner bar.

******

Tim Mulroney arrived at Micky's to find a locked door. It was no doubt strange, since the staff didn't even seem to bolt up the place after closing. It was a small town, and burglary was the last thing on anyone's mind. So he knocked. When the door opened, Tim was met by a friendly face, Doris, the sort of motherly figure he had come to know and love throughout the years. But on this night, Doris appeared panicked. As Tim Mulroney entered the establishment, he found out why it was that the woman seemed alarmed. As Tim filed into the bar, passing Doris, the hand with the knife came out of nowhere. So fast had it moved that Tim Mulroney didn't even have time to react. The only thing he felt was a sharp brush. It was then that he looked down at the pool of blood gathering quickly beneath him.

Tim Mulroney instinctively put his hands to his throat. As the life drained out of him, the car fanatic, the man who was trying to do his best in life, but whose demons quickly came back to haunt him, even for a fleeting moment, couldn't help but to think what a tragic mistake he made. If only he had listened to his inner self telling him to stay away from that place, he would be alive today.

Or maybe he would have gotten himself hit by a car on the way to the auto parts store one day. Whatever the case, Tim was gone, and wasn't nobody brining him back.

******

The alarm clock went off and the man slowly began to awake. He was a stranger in these parts, but he had a mission to do. Hence the early rising. He lit up a cigarette and inhaled deeply, feeling the smoke fill his lungs like a church-going man filling himself up with the Holy Spirit. The first smoke of the day was always the best, and this man enjoyed his morning cigarette as much as the next. As the man readied himself for yet another day, he knew this one would be special. This was the day he had been looking forward to for a long, long time. As he bent over the bed to pull on his boots, he paused momentarily, smiling to himself. *This was it*, he thought. *The moment you've been waiting for.*

The man then gathered up his belongings and headed out. There wasn't much, just his coat, smokes, dark shades and a foot-long blade that he kept on his person at all times.

Never know when you might need some protection,

especially around these desolate parts.

But protection was not what the stranger had on his mind

on this particular day. Revenge was.

Little Jimmy didn't deserve to die. He was just a boy for

Christ's sake. But the driver didn't take that into account on

that day.

The man missed his son dearly. Never stopped missing

him. Sure it had been three years, but a father's love for his

child never fades. And when that child dies so young and

so suddenly, it's as if the pain is a hundred times worse.

The stranger was initially going to forgive his son's killer.

But the trial's outcome proved that wasn't to be.

It was truly a disgrace, the sentence handed down by the

black robe-clad man who has the audacity to refer to

himself as judge. Forty eight months and community

service. For running down a little boy.

No. This father wasn't about to let that little mistake slide.

So he did what any father would do in his situation, at least a father whose grip on reality became slightly loosened with the daily reminder of a son in the grave. For this father took justice into his own hands.

******

The justice was swift and assured. When the man started to think this task wasn't for him, he pulled a picture of his boy out of his wallet. Things went smoother after that. His hand became steady, and his mind clear. The only thing he was dedicated to doing was avenging his son's death. He'll never forget the feeling of plunging a knife into the belly of another human being. *That drunk wasn't a human being*, the man would often tell himself, his mantra, if you will. This is what kept him going, allowing him to carry out the task. *This guy was a no-good, piece of shit, baby-killing drunk.*

The problem was that after the deed was done, the man was left feeling unsatisfied. He wasn't quite sure why. The scum who took away his boy was now gone, yet the feeling

92

of needing revenge remained ever-present.

Soon, the stranger decided to quench his thirst, and he set out to kill again. The thing about it was, killing just anyone didn't satisfy his craving. It was only those who reminded him of his son's killer, namely, boozers.

Pretty soon, this stranger from another town was carving a path of destruction across the country. Unfortunately for the patrons at a little watering hole called Micky's, their lives crossed paths with a man whose sensibilities had long gone out the window.

When the stranger pulled up to the bar, he had already made up his mind. It didn't take him long after that first sip of tonic water, (it's all he ever drank these days; he couldn't stand the thought of alcohol anymore), to decide this would be his last run.

After stabbing one customer in the back and slashing the throat of poor Tim Mulroney, the man suddenly felt a feeling of relief. He knew in his heart his work was now done. There was only one thing left to do.

The sound of the single shot echoed throughout the dingy bar. The sight of brain matter filled the room. The patrons who were left unscathed, at least physically, registered a state of shock. The carnage had only lasted a few moments from the moment the man stepped foot in the door, but the horrid act would no doubt leave a lasting impression on those unsuspecting innocents for years to come.

Doris quit the job. After taking some time off to collect her mental faculties, she landed a gig slinging booze to another local crowd at a family tavern.

For others, the whole experience turned them off to the drink all together. Johnny Bowers took to coffee instead. The thought that he could cross paths with another crazed madman who hated the sight and smell of booze was too much for him to bear. It's an understatement to say that the 35-year-old manual laborer was affected.

As for the stranger, his back story remained a mystery to the folks at Micky's. They never learned about his slain son, the kangaroo court, the revenge-killing. For all they knew, this man was a looney who happened to stumble upon a little bar in the woods. If it wasn't Micky's, it would have been someplace else.

But it *was* Micky's, the place where the stranger himself drew his last breath. He always knew it would end this way. He couldn't go on killing in this manner. The feeling of obsession was too much to bear.

It was only a .380 caliber, but it was enough to do the job. Just aim it at the right spot and all would be over soon enough.

And it was. That quickly. No more haunting thoughts of a child lost too early, a disgraceful justice system, a growing obsession. It was time to sleep now, he told himself. And boy did it feel good to rest.

Hunger

Sometimes it was the sound of a dripping faucet. Other times it was the feel of his favorite chair. What mattered here were not the specifics, but the mere fact that loneliness and isolation are what reminded Tony Grady of his problem.

You see, Tony was an alcoholic. Is an alcoholic. What do they say about this thing being a disease? That it's something you always have inside you, sort of like the herpes virus. It lies dormant, but certain external factors can trigger an outbreak.

For Tony Grady, being alone was the worst, for it was when he was alone that he enjoyed getting drunk. Why? Well for starters, there was nobody there to watch him, to look over his shoulder, to monitor how much he was drinking.

No. For Tony being alone was his most favorite time. It was when he could indulge his passion, which usually came in the form of a bottle of scotch. Or gin. Or vodka. Or brandy. Tony wasn't picky.

The thing of it, though, was that Tony wasn't really happy, and he hadn't been happy since his wife died. Shelley was the love of his life. The two met while both had been separately vacationing out west. Tony was on a backpacking trip conducting research for his latest novel, a story about a post-college grad who takes to the open road, and decides to set up camp at various wildlife refuges in the Pacific Northwest.

For Tony Grady, a Philly boy born and bred, hiking in unfamiliar terrain helped him formulate the backdrop of his writing project.

Shelley was the outdoorsy type, and the two crossed paths by mere happenstance.

Not that any of that matters now. After the accident, Tony swore off rock climbing for good. He could still hear his wife's screams. He can still recall, in vivid detail, the sound of the rope snapping, and his love tumbling down the side of that godforsaken jagged cliff, never to be seen again.

Tony Grady was a writer, so, needless to say, he always

enjoyed the drink. But after Shelley died, he hit the bottle pretty hard. It took a good two years for him to realize that his actions would lead to death in no uncertain terms. Actually, the real wake-up call was the near miss, (why do cops call it that?), involving his Jeep Wrangler and the black lab who darted out in front of him that mid-March day on a windy, rain-slicked road near his house.

Tony loved dogs, so quite naturally, the incident shook him up. Then and there Tony decided he needed to seek out help. And he did.

The meetings were awful, at least at first. All that talk about a higher power, and how one needed to accept certain things they couldn't change, and change only those things they could. How'd the rest go, "...and the wisdom to know the difference?"

Yeah, just what Tony Grady, failed writer and widower, needed. He could deal with his problem on his own, thank you very much. The real problem, however, and what Tony always knew deep down inside, was that he couldn't.

That's why Tony kept busy. He found that when his mind was occupied, and his hands had a task to do, he was less inclined to dwell on that feeling of wanting a drink.

Because after all, he still gets those feelings, up until this very day, but Tony has gotten to the point now where he is able to suppress the desire, and recognize it as just that – an urge, and one that will surely pass if given enough time.

But sometimes the urges are powerful, so much so that Tony has to stop what he's doing, take a deep breath and refocus.

Eventually, Tony found solace in the comfort of others, and after a two-month hiatus from what used to be those God awful AA meetings, Tony returned. And it's a good thing he did. For if he stayed away, he would have never met Grace.

The name alone conjured up a sense of serenity. Grace was his "saving Grace," Tony used to tell himself. After his wife died, Tony thought he could never love again. The sentiment was not uncommon; for most people who lose spouses, especially in such an untimely manner as was the case with Mrs. Grady, it's hard to open up, to feel, to love, to be loved. Tony was no different. But when he started conversing with Grace at the meetings in that dank church hall, a place he dreaded going since it had the air of misery and failure, things started to seem different. A once miserable, lonely, deprived Tony Grady began to improve. He started enjoying life again, seeing potential in the burgeoning relationship between himself and this new lady friend.

That's what Tony liked to call Grace – his "lady friend." Girlfriends were for middle-schoolers, he was fond of saying. A lady friend was a woman, and Tony Grady was in no way into little girls.

Eventually, Tony and Grace became a couple, and they did the things couples do; go to the movies, grab a bite to eat, sit at the park, visit pet stores and look at those little furry puppies through storefront windows.

Yep, it was a fairly normal relationship. But one thing Tony refused to do with his new companion was any type of outdoor activity. It only reminded him of Shelley, and the last thing Tony needed when trying to move on with his life was a momentary setback in the form of lingering memories.

Other than avoiding outdoor recreation, things were fairly normal for Tony and Grace. But normalcy can only last so long. When that feeling sets in – you know the feeling – where it seems as though things are at a standstill, that's when it's time to spice things up. Only in Tony's jaded, deluded, half-functioning mind, spicing things up took on a new meaning after he became a widower at such a young age. It was then that Tony found himself entering unchartered territory.

****

It's hard to pinpoint exactly when our dear old friend Tony Grady lost it. Some say it happened when his wife tumbled off that half-mile-high cliff, the sight of her contorting body bouncing off of each and every rock shelf as if it were a rag doll, forever etched into Tony Grady's psyche.

Others contend Tony truly lost it when he came to the realization that he could no longer imbibe. Coming to grips with the fact that he simply couldn't be a social drinker, the poison having a vice-like grip on him, forever changed Tony's way of thinking. Whereas he used to look forward to coming home, hitting the bottle, and forgetting his worries and drowning his sorrows, Tony eventually tapped into his rational side, and convinced himself that giving up the booze was for the best.

But just because he handed in the bottle didn't mean he got nothing in return, for Tony Grady soon developed a new addiction, a new drug to feed his insatiable appetite. He developed a taste for something he had never before known, that is until he grew closer and closer to Grace Bentley. It could be said that Tony Grady was now in an elite club, one whose membership is extremely limited, yet as old as time. Tony Grady, ladies and gentlemen, had entered an entirely new plane of existence, and there was no turning back. No turning back indeed.

****

"In here, darling," Tony called out to his newfound love. The man with the addiction problem was now head over heels, only the subject of his affection wasn't Grace – per se.

Tony sat at the table, eagerly awaiting the delectable treat he was about to bestow upon himself.

"Are you ready?" he called out to no one in particular. Months had passed since Tony felt that stagnant feeling, that feeling as though his new relationship was at a standstill. His fear of losing someone else he had grown close to morphed into paralysis. It got to the point where Tony would not only forgo trips to the outdoors; he couldn't even bring himself to take Grace out on dates. His lady friend would have to be satisfied with nights in – a newly released movie, a meal, a chat and a bottle of, uh, well, a can of soda or cup of coffee. (God, how Tony resented his predicament).

****

As Tony prepared himself for his meal on this night, all he could think about was the rush he got these days. The sudden burst of energy. The life he would feel growing inside him. The feeling was not unlike what he would experience during his drinking days. In a way, though, it could be said Tony Grady had ventured beyond the pleasures of intoxication. What used to be the rush he got from spirits was soon overpowered by a newfound passion, one that instilled in him a feeling far superior to anything he had ever felt before.

****

As Grace entered the dining room, Tony noticed something different about her. There was something missing. Something wasn't right. But what was it? The gaps in his memory these days were not serving Tony Grady well. What was going on inside his head?

But soon, it dawned on him, and Tony Grady snapped back to reality. At least his reality, which wasn't saying much these days.

Tony looked down at his hand, and there it was – the remote. Oh, how he had forgotten the whole story. How the remote came to be. But now he remembered. Wow. Tony Grady really was losing it.

He was able to think back on the day that he got the idea for the remote. It was an especially trying day for Tony Grady. You see, Grace was nagging way too much. Much more than normal. So he bit her. Literally. Right on the forearm. He just grabbed it and, well, there's no need to sugarcoat. Took a bite right out of her flesh. It was then and there that Tony Grady developed his new addiction. His newfound love.

As his mind wandered back to the present, Tony could feel his fingers moving across the remote. They were on the forward button now, and as he smoothly hit the accelerator, here came Grace. But she was anything but graceful.

****

As the motorized chair approached Tony, who was seated

at the head of the table, (as he always placed himself), he felt his mind begin to unravel. He tried to bring himself back to reality once again, (his reality, mind you, which is very different from ours), but the place he had gotten himself to was so far gone that there really was no turning back.

As Tony reached down to take Grace's hand, it suddenly dawned on him – he had that one last week. Silly Tony. *Go for the other one*, he told himself. But that, too, had already been consumed.

On this night, Tony would simply have to settle for whatever was left. But it was slim pickings. What was once a beautiful young lady full of hope, full of life, full of love, was now something vastly different. For Grace Bentley had been relegated to a new status. She belonged to Tony Grady now. She belonged inside him, feeding his body, mind and soul. It was ironic, but as her physical life was being slowly drained, Tony felt himself being slowly brought back to life. Tony Grady had a new addiction, alright. And there was no telling where his appetite would take him.

Delirium

The ticking sound the second hand made as it circled around the clock seemed to be magnified by a thousand, although he knew that was only his mind's interpretation. It was his keen sense of awareness, probably brought on by a forceful focus, that made the sounds emanating from the grandfather clock seem much louder than they actually were.

He wasn't always this focused, mind you. As a matter of fact, days, even hours earlier, it was almost as though he was a different person. But that's in the past; what's done is done. He's the one who made the decision, and he's the one who will have to live with it.

But still, one can't help but to wonder if things could have turned out differently if maybe … Oh, who was he kidding. This was a destiny he was fulfilling and he knew it. There was no lying to himself; he had been waiting for this moment for some time now, and there was no way he was turning back. *Get a grip*, he told himself. *Do what you set out to do.* That's it, all he needed was a little push. A little self-motivation. After all, without motivation, nobody would get anywhere in life. *That's all,* he thought, *I just need some motivation.* So he went and found it.

****

When he returned, he still found himself questioning how he got to this point. He was still unsure about the task he knew in his heart needed to be carried out. But why? Really, just what was it that was preventing him from doing what he knew had to be done? Was it society? Was he simply talking himself out of it? Was he a bit rusty? He didn't know. What he did know was that he needed to get over this hump and confront his fear head-on. If people never got over their fears, nothing would ever be accomplished in this world.

So again, it just came down to simple motivation. With that realization, he opted to do the only logical thing – he went out and got motivated ... again. But even then, he was feeling the same apprehension, experiencing the same unease. What he really needed to do was go and take his mind off of things. So he decided to grab a drink. Nothing takes the edge off like a good stiff one, and he knew this as well as anyone else. So that's exactly what he did. The problem was, he returned to discover nothing really changed. Why, he wondered. Just why was this thing so difficult. He'd done it before.

He decided to take a nap. While he slept, he thought all about Amy, what she had grown to mean to him. But Amy was gone, and there was no bringing her back. The sooner he realized this, the better off he would be. Continuing to think about the love of his life would only make the task at hand that much more difficult to accomplish. No. What he needed was some solid sack time without these intrusive thoughts. So he decided to get drunk ... again. After all, he never really seemed to dream when he was passed out cold from a night of heavy boozing. So drank is what he did. And that's the last thing he remembered.

****

When he awoke, a cold reality slapped him in the face: his

problem, much to his dismay, had not gone away. It was still right in front of him, mocking him. What, he thought, could possibly make things better? Booze didn't seem to do it, (a rare occurrence for him). And sleep wasn't helping in any way. No. The only thing left to do was to carry out the task. And he did.

It was difficult, at first, but after some time he got used to it. After all, there was no other way. This was it. This was the only answer. But just because he brought himself to do it didn't mean he could forget. There were good times. Like the love he once felt for Amy. It was true love; or so he thought. And all those great times they shared together. But good things don't last, and eventually it got to the point where the two simply didn't see eye to eye on a whole host of matters. It wasn't until the life began to grow inside Amy that he finally put his foot down. *There will be none of that*, he often told himself. *She's going to regret not listening to me this time.*

He knew it had to be done. How many times had he told

Amy there was no way in hell he was bringing a child into this shithole of a world. But she just didn't listen. Amy was selfish, is what she was. Things always had to go her way. Well, she made her bed. Now she can lie in it. And that's precisely how she ended up. Face up with the coldness of sharp metal having left its mark on the very spot in which the argument, the final one they had, mind you, first started.

****

Taking Amy and their unborn child out of this world didn't start as a conscious decision. The two had been arguing for weeks about this. She wanted to keep the baby; he knew better. Rearing a child in today's day and age was the last thing he was prepared to do. Willing to do. His woman just didn't feel the same way. Amy was all about having this kid, which undoubtedly made things even more difficult. It finally got to the point where he realized he wasn't going to win this argument. But not winning wasn't a choice. So he stacked the cards in his favor.

He had killed before, a little secret he kept hidden from

Amy. She never had any suspicions. After all, it's not like in the movies, where there are all these telltale "signs" that one's living with a killer.

Stanley Gruber wasn't a fictional character out of a movie or the pages of a storybook. He was real. He had a job. A mortgage. A life, it would seem, much like anyone else. But underneath there was a side to Stanley that only he knew of, one he kept all to himself. He even kept it from his love, Amy.

****

The first time he did it was in college. He had been dating a girl named Leah at the time. Her last name, he couldn't recall. What Stanley always did remember, however, was her mocking nature. After a good six months together, the couple had a blowout argument. It was then and there that Stanley lost his cool. It was also then and there that Stanley first developed a taste for the selfish act.

Taking one's life just didn't seem that hard for Stanley. Of course when the deed was done, he had to move away. And change his name. Stanley Gruber sounded inconspicuous enough.

Law enforcement never caught up with Stanley. He went on to live his life, only carrying out murder under the most called-for circumstances, at least in his warped little mind. At the time he met Amy, Stanley hadn't killed in many years. He lived a seemingly straight and narrow life. The only time he would take someone else's was when the situation truly demanded it. That was rare though.

****

The argument they had that morning started much like the others during the prior weeks, but this one was ramped up in intensity. Amy was tired of hearing Stanley go off about this world being unfit for a child. She wanted a baby oh so badly, and the fact that she was finally able to conceive meant a newfound hope for Amy, who, herself, had a difficult upbringing. She saw this as a chance to give another human being something she never had growing up – love and affection.

So needless to say, when Stanley began to start in with his diatribe, Amy was having none of it. But the last thing she expected was for things to get physical. After all, they never had before. Sure, they argued in the past. Every couple does as some point in the relationship. But physicality was a far-off notion. Stanley had never shown signs he could become abusive.

To Stanley, the ability to shut it on and off was his saving grace. That's why nobody ever suspected him of anything. It's almost as if he was born without a conscience. How else could his back-and-forth be explained? After the death of that bitch Janice Goodman the decade before, the cops did question Stanley. But he remained cool under pressure. He was even able to whip up some fake emotions. *God, this is easy*, Stanley thought.

And it seemed to get easier as time went by. Perhaps that's the reason Stanley had no qualms at all about removing his unborn child from Amy's womb.

****

When Amy awoke, all she could sense was an inability to move. And sadness, betrayal and helplessness, of course.

I warned you it would come to this, but you just never listened.

The words were in Stanley's mind, not spoken out loud, of course. But to Stanley they were a viable means of communication. It didn't matter that he was uttering insanities to himself. There would have been no changing his mind even if he had been conversing audibly. Stanley's depravity had developed throughout the years to the point where nothing would cure him. There was no help for Stanley Gruber. It's just a shame poor Amy had come into his life. She deserved better than this. Having it all end this way. She was a sweet girl, with a life full of promise. Now she existed as half a woman. The baby that was growing inside of her was no more. Her life was no more. It was so unfair that Stanley Gruber got to go on and live his life. It's not a stretch to say he would commit a similar crime somewhere down the road. Men like Stanley Gruber don't get cured. They're incapable of change despite beliefs to the contrary. Sometimes they don't get stopped either. That's the way it goes though. And it will always be that way.

****

As Stanley Gruber stood over his deceased Amy, the result of their lovemaking lying next to her lifeless corpse, the man who tried his hand at a happy life couldn't help but to think maybe he was destined to become the depraved individual into which he had evolved. Maybe this was fate, Stanley told himself.

But how much longer could he go on like this? When would his madness end?

These were questions to which he didn't have answers. The focus now was on the present. And it was at that moment that Stanley Gruber saw her walking by. The young woman who had just moved into the house down the street. Stanley just had to know her name. But he would have to clean up his place a bit before he asked her over for a drink.

Interrupted

Mandy Bennett didn't like basements.

Her aversion to the dank, bottom spaces was likely traced to the fact that she never lived in a house that had one, being that she grew up in a beach town. You know, building code regulations and all.

That all changed, though, after she married Jerry.

The two purchased a beautiful cabin-like home on a desolate tract of land in upstate Pennsylvania, a far cry from what Mandy was accustomed to.

Her childhood home at the beach had no basement. Neither did the city apartments in which she dwelled up until the point she met and married Jerry, who, unlike his new bride, enjoyed spending countless hours in a structure's lowest floor.

You see, Jerry was a hobbyist, and his pastimes always required ample space with which to work, and basements seemed to afford him the roominess he required.

One reason the couple chose the cabin home in rural Susquehanna County, just over the border from New York

State, was that it had a basement that was, at least in Jerry's words, "to die for."

****

"Oh, come on, sweetie. This place is perfect!"

Jerry had pleaded with his new bride to buy the house. It had sprawling acreage, a country feel, a cozy vibe. And most of all, a spacious basement that would be conducive to Jerry's needs. This place was it. Jerry just knew it in his heart.

"Well, alright," Mandy told him, not realizing at the time that she was making her new husband the happiest man alive. "But you owe me ... big time."

Jerry promised to help keep the place clean, cook meals from time to time. Really, help out in any way he could. Prior to the home purchase, the two resided in a cramped, one-bedroom apartment in New York City.

Mandy didn't mind. Jerry hated it.

The plan was always to move back to Pennsylvania, Jerry's home state, since most of his family still lived there, and

Mandy, well, she really had no family left, so it didn't much matter to her where they lived.

They had been planning to start a family, and it made more sense for the couple to be around Jerry's parents so help would be nearby if they ever needed it.

Yep. Kids were definitely in the cards, but the couple wanted to get settled into a house before they welcomed little ones into the world.

The day that the two moved into their new house was as normal as any other. But things didn't stay that way for long. It all started with the whimpering.

****

"Jerry, sweetie. Do you hear that?"

Mandy's calls to her husband were met with silence. She was unaware he had taken a trip to the store.

Jerry was a model train enthusiast. He developed an affinity for the hobby as a young boy.

He never had many friends so playing with toy trains is how he spent most of his time. He just couldn't seem to kick the habit.

Even with a beautiful new wife at home, Jerry often seemed to spend more time indulging his pastime than "indulging" in his bride.

The sound was coming from the basement. Great. The one place Mandy felt uncomfortable investigating.

The couple had lived in the home for about two months when Mandy started hearing strange sounds emanating from down below.

They were whimpering sounds. Almost like a sick animal that had found its way into the home's lower floor and took refuge.

In her old life, Mandy worked in advertising for a big, New York City firm.

Jerry was a writer and artist, so he spent most of his time at home, where he kept an office.

In the Brooklyn apartment, his workspace was the living room, if you could call it that.

In the new house, he set up shop in the basement.

After moving to the country, Mandy decided to be a stay-at-home wife, most likely in preparation for the baby.

She was still physically able to work, being that the life inside of her had only been growing for six weeks or so by this point. But she wanted to properly prepare for motherhood, so full-time home confinement is what she opted for.

Mandy didn't mind; she had been working since she was a teenager, and a little break would do her some good.

Jerry was actually a fairly successful author, so the two were able to live off of his income.

The royalties that were coming in from a children's book series that Jerry hit it big with helped pay the bills.

And the couple had some decent savings to fall back on, so money wasn't really ever an issue.

Jerry also had a freelance writing business, mostly doing copywriting for ad agencies, a lucrative gig to say the least. Mandy, who wasn't really used to depending on a man, finally allowed herself to be taken care of. And it felt nice for a change.

She had been enjoying her time as a jobless woman, and even though Jerry worked at home, the found they each had the space they needed; the house was huge, and both Jerry and Mandy were able to retreat to their respective corners when needed.

Mandy felt quite comfortable in the house – that is until the whimpering started.

The first day she heard the disconcerting noise, Mandy wrote it off to her mind playing tricks on her. Either that or it was coming from outside the home.

She was still uncomfortable with basements, so she decided to ignore the sounds; she didn't want to have to venture down there.

Yup. Ignorance was the best policy in this case. So she let it go.

****

The strange sounds that appeared to be coming from the basement soon subsided, and life returned to normal.

Another month or so passed without the occurrence of anything out of the ordinary.

Jerry continued with his writing projects. Mandy spent her days preparing the baby's room.

All in all, life seemed good, or at least normal.

Then one night, Mandy was awoken from a deep sleep. It was screeching sounds from the basement that did it.

"Jerry, wake up. Did you hear that?"

Jerry relished his sleep. Needless to say, being woken up at 2:30 in the morning was not a pleasant experience.

"I don't hear anything, sweetie. Go back to sleep. You were probably just dreaming."

"I *was* just dreaming. That's the problem. It was a good dream and I'd like to get back to it."

Jerry wasn't winning this one, so, in an effort to appease his wife, he grabbed his pistol and ventured down the creaky stairs to the basement to check things out.

As he was making his way down, Jerry couldn't help but to think that his wife was probably just hormonal or something. Call it a case of the pregnancy crazies.

Either way, a happy wife was a happy husband, so he got his ass out of the warm bed and went to do her bidding.

"There's nothing down here, babe!," Jerry called up to his wife.

To his surprise, Jerry turned around to see Mandy at the top of the basement stairs.

"What's going on down here," Mandy said. "What the hell is all this."

"Uh, Mandy. I can explain."

"Explain?" Mandy shot back. "How the hell are you going to explain all this?"

What Mandy saw shocked her conscience. Cages upon

cages filled with animals. Sick, helpless and tortured

animals.

Some with missing limbs. Others with singed fur. Still

others with hollowed-out eye sockets.

The carnage was sickening.

"Jesus, Jerry. How could you! These poor things. What are

you some sick bastard?!"

"Mandy, just calm down. I don't know what you're…,"

But Mandy wouldn't let her husband finish. He had done

enough and it was time for her to speak.

"Is this what you've been doing with your time? Torturing

innocent creatures?"

Jerry tried to explain. He tried to tell his wife that all he did

was spend way too much money on model train parts. After

all, that's what he assumed her reaction was about.

There were no cages. No sick and tortured animals. No

carnage.

There was only a fortune in model train parts and accessories lining the cold basement.

But Mandy's cabin fever had gotten the best of her. The pregnancy. The isolation. These were things Mandy thought she could handle, but obviously couldn't.

To Mandy, however, the sights, sounds and smells of half-dead animals were as real as anything else.

It's just sad that it all had to end this way. There had been so much promise at one point.

The stress of her acute psychological trauma caused Mandy to lose the baby.

The acute soon morphed into the chronic, and she was never the same again.

It was hard for Jerry to commit his wife. But it was necessary. She needed the professional help offered by those in white coats. There was no getting better on her own.

Visiting his wife in a state institution wasn't easy, but Jerry forced himself to do it – month in, and month out.

When it appeared her condition was likely permanent, Jerry had his lawyer draft up the papers.

He would miss being married, but he missed having a coherent wife even more.

Jerry wished things turned out differently. He wished the couple had a chance at a normal life.

But normal isn't always meant to be.

For Jerry, the only thing that brought some peace of mind was the knowledge that his soon-to-be-ex-wife was once again living in a place without a basement.

He just wished Mandy was well enough to realize it.

The
Unforgiving

When you get right down to it, an innate curiosity is what most likely led Chase Branson to become a newspaper reporter. Unfortunately, in the end, it was that very same desire to satisfy his own urges that got him killed. But more on that later. Let us start from the beginning.

Our tale of longing and obsession takes foot in the suburbs of Philadelphia, Pennsylvania, an area of the country that has many ghosts. Not necessarily the ones that make up tall tales and scary movies, (although you'll soon come to find that the line between fact and fiction is indeed sometimes blurred), but rather ghosts in the figurative sense.

You see, our friend Chase was born and raised in these parts, and like many who are native to a specific locale, the beauty and charm of an area are often lost on those who take their hometown for granted.

As for Chase, he could be described as a real go-getter professionally, although he was a rather quiet and introverted fellow, which was somewhat antithetical to the job he had to perform, what with dealing with the public and all. But he seemed to perform his duty perfectly fine, and seldom were there any complaints, at least not from those with whom he worked. In fact, he was never really one to have a bad word said about him, which couldn't be said for all those employed in the lively newsroom at the paper. Some days it seemed to be gossip central.

Yep, Chase Branson was well liked; he just didn't say much. And although people weren't his strong suit, he was perfectly capable of putting on his professional cap and dealing with them when the situation called for it.

Before we fast-forward to those fateful couple of days, it's important to note that Chase started to change a bit in the few weeks leading up to the big incident. It all started with a rare show of emotion on the part of our young reporter, accompanied by a very rare display of verbal frustration.

"Well for Christ's sake, Bill. Why is this assignment different than any other I've undertaken in the three goddam years I've been under your employ?"

Chase's comments, and certainly unexpected tone, took his

editor aback.

Bill Witherly had been the executive editor of The Gazette for ten years. In that time, he had dealt with some brash, young reporters, but most of them were hired with that no-nonsense attitude. In fact, that's probably why they got the job in the first place.

But someone like Chase Branson was different. It was strange seeing his demeanor change almost overnight. And to think, it had to do with a mere story, one that Bill didn't even think was all that worth pursing.

Specifically, the situation had to do with an old historic house that was in danger of being torn down. Although the home hadn't been occupied for many years, word was that some in town wanted to save the old place while the county had its sights set on demolishing it.

For Chase, however, the situation wasn't about land preservation, or even getting the scoop on what was sure to be a big story. (The house was reputed to have once been home to Gen. George Washington himself).

No. For Chase Branson, going after this story had become an obsession. The problem was that nobody knew why it became so important to him to write about the old structure, which physically wasn't even all that impressive. Not when you compare it to some of the other historic buildings in the area.

It can be said that young Chase's life had taken a turn for the worse once he started looking in to that old place. He just didn't realize it at the time.

****

It all started on a day not unlike any other. Chase had left for work that morning feeling pretty much the same way he always did; lonely, would be a good description as any, although not in a depressing sense. You see, Chase cherished his solitude, he was able to focus more this way on the things that mattered most to him, and at this stage of his life it was his career that took precedence.

After leaving his one-room, downtown city apartment, Chase hopped the commuter rail, just as he always did, and headed into the office. But on this day, for some strange reason or another, he decided to get off at the stop before his usual drop-off point. It was a crisp, fall morning, and our friend desired to walk that extra mile or so.

On his way in, Chase opted to duck into a café momentarily and grab a cup of coffee for the balance of the stroll.

"They ought not touch the thing, no sir. They ought leave that old place alone. Don't they know what happens when you go stickin' your nose where it don't belong?"

The voice, old and crackled, came from a corner table in the rear of the small coffee shop. For some reason, Chase was drawn to it. He couldn't just get his hot beverage and hit the road. No. Our reporter was the curious type, and he smelled a story, even in that brief, fleeting moment. So he turned around, and caught the old fellow's eye.

" … pay for that?"

Chase suddenly snapped back to reality. "I'm sorry?"

"I said, aren't you going to pay for that?" asked the counter worker, who seemed as though he was annoyed enough at the world simply for having to work in the place. He didn't need any more excuses to be in a foul mood.

"Oh, of course," Chase said, reaching into his pocket. "Sorry about that. I seem to be a little distracted this morning."

After he paid, Chase made his way to the back of the room. As he got closer to the table where the voice had come from, he noticed that the old man was sitting all alone. He must have been talking to himself. And while Chase usually preferred to stay away from these strange types, he found himself uncontrollably drawn to the man.

"Excuse me," Chase said, as courteously as possible. "I couldn't help but to overhear. Did you say something about some old place being in danger?"

The old man answered the young reporter, but strangely enough, he never made eye contact. It didn't matter, though. His tone was directive enough.

Again, Chase pressed the old man. "Sir. Not to be rude, but did I hear you talking about an old building? The reason I ask is that I'm a reporter, and recently there has been talk

of the county wanting to knock down the old …"

But Chase never finished. The old man simply cut him off,

and launched into some rant about how people should

respect the dead because they're not really dead, or

something along those lines. The reporter didn't really

follow, but let the old guy finish nonetheless.

"You see, the dead need a place to live too, you know," the

old man continued. "For the dead are just as alive as you

and I. No sir, they ought leave that place well alone."

"Sir, is the place you're talking about the one over by the

railroad tracks that may be demolished? The place they say

George Washington once lived in?"

But there was no point in prodding any further. The old

man simply said his piece, and then dropped his head to the

table, as if he tired himself out with just that little bit of

conversation. If you could call it conversing.

So Chase, coffee in hand, and satchel slung over his

shoulder, once again took to the streets. He had about

another half-mile to go to the newsroom, and his mind was now fully engaged. It had been one strange morning, but this was just the beginning. Things were about to get a whole lot stranger.

The next few days were difficult for Chase to get through. While he had other stories to work on, he just couldn't stop thinking about the old house, not to mention the old man in the coffee shop. Something strange was going on, and young Chase was desperate to find out just what it was.

Mid-week, Chase finally had some down time and decided to stop by the local library. He decided that while no one else, including his editor, saw a particularly interesting story in the ill-fated house, this reporter was determined to prove everyone wrong. That notion was solidified after Chase found what he was looking for.

While perusing the stacks, Chase came across a book on local folklore. And while he was never much for hocus pocus, the more he read, the more credence he put into the stories about the old house.

In addition to the book, Chase came across some old newspaper clippings. One told the story of how the infamous house came to be without any owners during the past few years, something Chase had become more and more curious about. According to the news accounts, the house was lived-in up until a decade or so ago, but became vacant after the tragic circumstances surrounding the deaths of the last family who called the place home.

The details were murky, but the grisly scene depicted in the paper told of a charnel house, what appeared on the surface to be a murder suicide case, but was never officially proven as such during the course of the investigation. Apparently, the authorities decided to close the book on the case since there were no witnesses, and all persons involved were deceased, leading the case to be built upon pure guesswork. The weird thing, and what certainly stood out in Chase's mind, was that the family who occupied the home at the time seemed perfectly normal. Police found nothing out of the ordinary about the husband, wife and their two kids.

Along the way, however, something changed. In the months leading up to their deaths, the family became very reclusive, shunning life outside of the house. The only time the parents would leave – and toward the end, it was really only the husband who stepped outside the walls – was to get groceries. But they didn't really speak to anyone, and friends and neighbors who got along perfectly well with them in the past started to become worried.

The children, who were still young when they met their ill-fated demise, were hardly ever seen outside of the home in those last few months.

In the end, everyone seemed to have his or her own take on what happened to the family. Some believe that an ancient evil was awakened in the house and took out its revenge on the occupants. And still others believe one of the parents, most likely the father, (the wife was apparently the submissive type, at least according to those who came across her), simply went crazy, and took the other family members out of this world in the cruelest of ways.

Research like this would have most people running in the opposite direction of that old place, but Chase Branson wasn't most people. In fact, reading the old accounts only aided his quest to find out what really happened in that house, and why some wanted it torn down. Chase was armed with a bit of knowledge, and he was ready to find out just what goes on behind those walls. But our young reporter failed to take one thing into account, and that's what happened to the cat whose curiosity got the best of him.

****

The air was crisp and sunrays shone through the windows, just enough to give off a little early-morning warmth, and not enough to be annoying. Yep. Autumn was beautiful around these parts, and the climate made it that much easier for our young friend to get out of bed and start his workday.

But these days, Chase didn't need any help getting motivated. His research into the old house was beginning to finally come together, and who knows, he just might have a

nice story on his hands, one, that if read by enough people,

could have an effect on the ill fate awaiting the old

structure. The funny thing was, Chase didn't even know

why he wanted to save the dilapidated place. It's not like he

was some sort of history buff. And besides, with what

happened in that old place, it was a wonder it hadn't been

torn down years before. Somewhere along the way, he

guessed, it just got passed over by local preservationists.

Interestingly enough, while the place could undoubtedly be

considered conservation-worthy, due to its age and

reputation alone, it had never been placed on any type of

historic register. Chase, being the quasi-conspiracy theorist

that he was, wondered if politics had anything to do with it.

They always seemed to play a part in something, and he

wouldn't be surprised if that were the case here.

That theory was solidified after the clever reporter

discovered that somewhere along the line, the home was

owned by a once prominent local family, the Bells.

According to some newspaper accounts he read, the patriarch at the time, Thomas Bell, was reputed to have gone crazy. Nobody knows for sure what caused his apparent madness, but he wound up being committed to an insane asylum. The strange thing was, his family, a wife and two kids, were never to be seen or heard from again. The story went that his wife awoke one morning to find her husband in the midst of some strange rant about the basement of their home talking to him. Not surprisingly, she called their doctor. Long story short, Thomas was locked away in some institution, where he rocked away the rest of his days in a wicker chair doped up on benzodiazepines. And what became of his wife and children is still not known. One day they were there, and the next they were gone. Simple as that.

The house sat unoccupied for many years, that is until the most recent family moved in. Their stay, as Chase had already learned, was cut short.

Through his research, Chase discovered that the town's

current mayor had connections to the Bell family. Chase was still unsure of the exact relationship, but his sources – confidential ones of course – never told a lie.

During his time as a reporter, Chase was able to cultivate the types of relationships many journalists only dream about. It was here that he got many of his story leads, and also many of his confirmations, which beforehand would be mere conjecture.

But while Chase was certain the mayor had ties to this family with a strange past, he was still unsure of what this had to do with the deaths, which occurred many years after the Bells resided there. One thing was for sure – Chase was going to make the connection, and this beautiful fall day was as good as any to get started.

First stop was Tobin Mansfield's. The old man had a charm Chase could only equate to old world etiquette; truthfully, the old timer had a dapper English accent, and that was enough for the young reporter.

Tobin was the head of the local historical society, and in

addition to being a very well informed resident, he was just an all-around nice guy. His wife had passed away a few years back, and Chase would make sure to stop by at least once a week to see how the old man was holding up. In the beginning, Chase simply used the old man as a source, as cold as that sounds. He had been around long enough, and seemed to have a pretty good knowledge of what was going on around town, so the young reporter would use this to his advantage.

But somewhere along the way, Tobin grew on Chase, and the two seemed to become friends.

"Mr. Mansfield. Mr. Mansfield, are you in there?"

Even though the old man told Chase time and time again to forgo knocking, and just come in if the foyer light was on, the world-weary reporter just couldn't bring himself to enter without an invite.

"Mr. Mansfield, I need to talk to you about ..."Chase was cut short.

The door opened, and standing in the doorway was an old

man who resembled a cross between Donald Pleasence,
you know, the actor who played the shrink from the
'Halloween' film series, and Wilford Brimely, the guy from
the Quaker Oats commercials.

"Listen, Mr. Mansfield, I need to talk to you about ..."

Again he was cut off.

"Son, how many times do I have to tell you to call me
Tobin. Now, what seems to be troubling you?"

Somewhere deep down inside, Chase had wished the old
man hadn't asked him that. It would have made him feel a
lot more at ease.

"Well, where should I start?"

"From the beginning would be nice."

"Right. Mr. Mansfield ... uh, Tobin. How much do you
know about the old house in town that people are saying
will be demolished? I've found out a little bit about the old
place, through research and talking to others who have been
in town as long as you. No offense intended, of course."

"None taken."

"So, what do you know? Is it really the shadowy place people make it out to be?"

The old man looked as though the young reporter caught him by surprise. Nevertheless, he was never one to shy away from controversy; Chase later came to find out that Tobin Mansfield himself was one hell of a newspaper reporter in his day.

"Chase, why don't you have a seat. I'll go grab some coffee."

The reporter no doubt had his fill of caffeine for the day, but he wasn't about to turn down a chance to hear what the old man had to say.

After what seemed like an eternity, Tobin returned to his sitting room, coffee carafe in one hand, scrapbook in the other. Just the thought of the old man actually knowing something about this whole situation got Chase excited.

"So," the old man dropped the scrapbook onto to the table, "what do you want to know?"

****

The normally un-phased reporter looked bewildered. He learned some stuff about the old house, all right, but was disappointed to find out that everything the old man told him was, as they say in the newspaper business, strictly off the record. It turned out that some weird shit had gone down in that place over the years, and somehow the mayor's ancestors had something to do with it. Of course, what would be the modern day Bell family no longer went by that surname – after the bizarre incident with old Thomas, the family had changed it. Chase couldn't blame them; if something that strange had happened in his lineage, he surely would have opted for a new identity as well.

But it was definitely the same family. Chase wanted to confront the mayor, but didn't know how. No matter how he approached it, the mayor would surely brush the young reporter aside, chalking it up to youthful eagerness. Besides, what would Chase say: *Listen, I know who you are. I know where you come from. And I know your family has covered up a huge secret for many years.*

That surely wasn't going to cut it. The mayor is in a position of power, and with power comes the best PR money can buy. But Chase didn't want to deal with a public relations lapdog. He wanted to talk to the man himself. He wanted to ask him, why? Why would the mayor be ashamed of his family roots? Just because something bad happened somewhere down the family tree didn't mean he was to blame. It wasn't his fault, what happened those many years ago. But the thing Chase really wanted to know, the aspect of this whole thing that really bothered him, was why the mayor, presuming that's who was behind this, and Chase had no doubt it was, would want to keep the old house from being demolished? Wouldn't he want to rid the world of that awful structure? If the mayor was ashamed about what happened, he sure wasn't showing it by working to keep that place standing.

There had to be more to the story. But this was as far as Chase would get with the old man. He gave him all he

161

could, which at least was a good start. Chase thanked the old man, and walked out, scrapbook and all. Tobin Mansfield, being the consummate gentleman that he was, even let the young reporter take the newspaper clippings and notes with him, as long as he promised to return the items whenever he finished with them.

So that was that. Chase had what he needed to make some headway. Nothing would stop him now. Or so he thought.

****

Betty Mills typically had a friendly enough demeanor, so when Chase stopped by to see the mayor, and his secretary was short, he figured something was wrong.

"I'm sorry, Mr. Branson. Mr. Todd simply can't be bothered now. You'll have to come back another time."

"Well, could you just tell him it's important, and that I'm on deadline?"

Saying you're on deadline usually does the trick for a reporter looking to talk to someone, and it typically worked for Chase, but he didn't seem to be getting anywhere on this day. Ms. Mills seemed to be in no mood, and there was no way Chase was going to bust down the solid, oak door outside the mayor's office just to make himself known. So Chase left his card – the mayor no doubt had fifty copies, but Chase just got in the habit of handing them out wherever he went – and said he'd stop back another time. It's funny, but as Chase was walking out of the office, he could have sworn he heard Ms. Mills buzz into the mayor's office on the phone's intercom and say something about "that local reporter asking about an old house."

Something was going on, and Chase Branson didn't like it when things seemed out of place. He was after one thing, the truth, and if he wasn't going to make headway with the mayor, he'd simply try somewhere else. That's when Johnny Devoe came to mind.

******

"Johnny. It's Chase Branson. Listen, I've got something I need to talk to you about. Can you meet me at the café sometime this week? I think I've got one hell of a story on

163

my hands, and it involves your friend Julian Todd."

Johnny Devoe was the former mayor who lost to Julian Todd during the previous election. The two had a bitter race, one which Johnny has always maintained was tainted by bribes and dirty politics. It was no secret in town that there was no love lost between these two.

Chase always got along well with Johnny Devoe. He was young, at least for someone holding public office, he lived in the town practically his whole life, and, perhaps most important to Chase, he was forthcoming. His office was always open, and if the young reporter had questions, the former mayor always invited him in.

It was different with Mayor Todd. He seemed to conduct business behind closed doors. And while most of the time he came off as accommodating, there was something Chase didn't trust about the man, and it all seemed to stem from the allegations that surfaced about Todd cheating in the mayors' race. It was rumored that Todd somehow bought his way into office, but this could never be proven. Chase, and the reporter who preceded him, certainly tried their best, but to no avail.

So it stood to reason that when Chase dropped by with questions surrounding the old house, which had the makings of a potentially unfavorable story toward the current mayor, given his apparent connection to it, he would be turned away as swiftly as he was.

"What's going on, Chase. Is everything alright?" came the response on the other end of the phone.

The reporter seemed to have drifted off momentarily; he had been doing this a lot lately.

"Johnny. Have you heard anything about an old, historic house in town that may get torn down? There's been talk of this controversial move around here lately, and I thought word might have made it out your way."

A longtime resident, Johnny actually moved away after his defeat, not that far, but far enough that he didn't have to be under the jurisdiction of his crooked opponent.

"No. Why, what's going on?"

"Well, let's just say I have a hunch your old friend is up to no good, and it involves one of the oldest buildings in town."

Chase proceeded to tell Johnny the whole story. About the house, its strange history, the old man in the coffee shop, Tobin Mansfield, everything.

"Something's not right here, Johnny. And while I can't prove anything yet, I think Todd wants to keep this house standing, but I don't' know why. Maybe he has some financial stake in it."

To Chase, Mayor Todd seemed one to get involved in something strictly for monetary benefit; he sure didn't seem the type to want to restore an old building for its historical value.

"Look, can we meet up sometime? I want to show you some of these newspaper clippings I got from Mansfield."

"Alright." Johnny Devoe was always receptive. That was one of the qualities Chase liked about him. Even during the days when he was mayor, Johnny always dropped everything to help Chase. "Give me an hour. I'll meet you at the coffee shop."

******

It was around three o' clock by the time Chase met up with Johnny Devoe. The former mayor hopped off the train and the two headed over to a mutually favorite spot – the coffee shop where they met many times before to discuss local issues during Johnny's mayoral tenure.

"Listen, Chase. I'm just gonna come out and say it: I lied to you on the phone. I do know about the house, and let me just tell you, there's much more to this thing than you know."

Chase knew he chose the right person in Johnny Devoe. The guy always came through.

"But Chase, everything I'm gonna' tell you, well, it'll be near impossible to prove. Trust me, I've tried."

"Well," Chase replied, "I guess you'll just have to start from the beginning."

What followed was a strange tale that seemed more out of

an episode of The Twilight Zone than anything that could remotely resemble a factual story. Johnny began to tell the reporter, (off the record, as always), the real circumstances behind his election defeat. You see, Johnny knew all about the old Washington house. In fact, Julian Todd sort of ran on the platform of historic preservation, something that, oddly enough, Chase had forgotten about. He wasn't covering the local government beat at the time, (he had been assigned strictly to education reporting), but surely he should have remembered hearing all about how Todd's regular talking points at the time dealt with preserving the town as is so future generations could have something to be proud of. Now that he thought about it, Chase probably just wrote this off at the time to mere rhetoric from someone who wanted to hold public office.

But the story got weirder. As Johnny told it, the reason Julian Todd felt so strongly about that house was because his family had a history there, a rather sordid one. Apparently, even before his ancestors the Bells resided there, Todd had other ancestors who occupied the house. As the tale goes, the patriarch was shunned by society after it was rumored that he took part in rather bizarre rituals in the basement of the home.

Well, one night, after a passerby noticed smoke coming from the basement windows, the man was discovered. Thinking the family was in trouble, and the house was on fire, men stormed inside, only to discover the man engaged in a sickening act.

"You sure you want to hear this, man," Johnny asked.

Chase just stared at him with an expression that said *don't be ridiculous, you asshole. I didn't ask you here for nothing.*

Well, apparently the man was found to be on the dank basement floor, surrounded by candles, engaged in some sort of sex act with what could only be described as a hideous beast. When they came across the disturbing scene, the men grabbed the homeowner, took him outside, and burned him alive as a heretic.

The story had apparently survived to this day, strictly through word of mouth, and only among those familiar with local folklore. Chase never knew his friend the former mayor knew so much about this old place, and as he understood it now, for good reason.

****

"Listen, Bill. I can't really get into it right now. All I'm saying is you have to believe me. I've got one hell of a story on my hands."

Chase decided to call into the newsroom on this day; if he showed up, he knew his editor would put him on some other assignment, one, our young reporter knew, would be nothing compared to this gem he stumbled upon.

"Look, Bill, you're just going to have to trust me."

"Listen, kid. If you don't come in today, I hate to say it, but I'm gonna have to let you go. Even I've got a boss to answer to, Chase, and he's not pleased with where you've been putting your focus as of late."

Chase knew Bill was bluffing. There was no way his editor

and friend would fire him, especially over this. No. Chase Branson knew he was onto something, he just had to have his editor's trust.

"Bill, I understand the position you're in, and I'm sorry. But right is right. I know there's something going on with that house. I just have to find out what it is. I'm almost there, Bill. I just need a little more time. I'm really sorry." With that, Chase hung up the phone. He had never hung up on anyone before, especially not the person who signs his paychecks. But if he was going to find out what was really going on with this house, he had to give the situation his full attention. And he very well wasn't going to be able to do that while working on other, sub-par stories. So, for the first time in his life, Chase decided to take the road less traveled. Unfortunately, by the time he realized he should have listened to his editor, it was too late.

****

Chase Branson liked the nighttime. There was something peaceful about the darkness that appealed to someone of his nature. Maybe it was the fact that most everyone else was at home asleep, something that played to his introverted favor. Or maybe it had something to do with the fact that he was able to actually think, without the distractions of everyday life coming at him full force.

Whatever it was, Chase knew one thing; if he was going to get some work done, it had to be during this time of day. And so he ventured off.

No train was running at this time, so Chase opted to shuck out a few bucks for a cab. The driver gave him a look that said *what is a person like you doing traveling to the burbs in the middle of the night*, but Chase never gave it two thoughts.

After paying the man, the young reporter took to the streets. It would be another mile or so up the road to the old house, but Chase preferred to take the final leg of the journey on foot. He didn't want to chance anyone seeing him approaching the place, since it was supposed to be condemned, and off limits to passersby – especially young, nosy reporters.

For a fleeting moment, when Chase finally arrived at the place, he had what some would call moment of clarity, something inside his head telling him to abandon this visit, to forget the whole thing.

But Chase wasn't the type to let anything deter him from his ultimate objective, especially not in this type of situation. He knew there was more behind the push to save this old place – he just had to prove it. Well, hopefully a stroll through the house, or what the cops would no doubt call trespassing, would aid him in his quest. If only there was something inside that would offer some type of clue. Chase knew he had to go inside, and that's exactly what he did.

****

"Hello. Is anybody here?"

As if someone would be caught dead inside this old, musty place. Maybe he called out in fear, thinking he would stumble across a squatter, or some young teenagers looking for a place to get high, or make out, or both. Whatever it was, his call was met with nothing but an echoed, hollow response. Good. At least it made him feel better. You see, unlike many people, Chase wasn't afraid to be alone, even if it was in the confines of a creaky old house where some horrible things were reputed to have happened. Chase was more afraid of real things, like war, and government overreaching. This old place was cakewalk.

But as he made his way inside, Chase Branson, who generally let nothing faze him, felt overcome by a strange sensation. It was almost as if something was telling him to go deeper inside, down to the basement.

Undeterred, Chase pressed on. First, he walked through the ground floor, looking around for anything that might constitute as evidence. The home, for being so historic, was really rather unremarkable. Sure, it had nice hardwood floors, a good solid foundation, and other pleasing characteristics, and the layout was something unlike the cookie-cutter homes of today could offer, but aside from those noteworthy attributes, the place did not come across as all that special.

As he ventured up the stairs, Chase thought he heard some sounds emanating from the basement, but wrote it off as his mind playing tricks on him. He kept telling himself that he was the only one in this place, and for another brief moment, he began to ask himself why.

When he got to the top floor, Chase came to the realization that what they said was true: people really were a lot shorter years ago, the low ceiling a testament to how far we've come on the evolutionary scale. There were two bedrooms; one, quite clearly the master suite, if you can call the small space that, and the other a smaller room that would have been perfect for children.

As he made his way around, Chase realized he wasn't going to find anything here. There seemed to be nothing out of the ordinary, at least not that he could tell. And Chase had a pretty good nose for something being out of place.

Nothing jumping out at him, the reporter decided to check out the basement, or what he imagined would be nothing but a cramped, wine cellar. After all, that seemed to be the lower floor of choice for homebuyers during those days. When he got back to the main floor, Chase was once again overcome with an odd feeling, something he just couldn't shake. It was almost as if something was pulling at him, wanting him to see more.

He finally located the basement door, and ventured downstairs. Much to his dismay, the area was much as he imagined; a very tiny cellar that clearly couldn't have been home to the strange happenings Chase was told of. Weird sex acts, come on. This place was barely big enough to hold one person. And where were these so-called windows those men so many years ago supposedly saw smoke pouring from. There weren't any windows here, at least none that this observant newspaper reporter could locate. Feeling like he hit a dead end, Chase decided he saw enough, and was about to retreat. But just as he started venturing back upstairs, Chase heard a sound. Yes, it was definitely noise, he just couldn't place it. He had been halfway up the stairs when he told himself he had to go back down.

As he made his way around the cellar once again, the sounds became stronger, more pronounced. He finally was able to pinpoint where the sounds seemed to be emanating from, which seemed to be under the stairs. As he made his way around, he noticed a small doorway, almost the size of the entranceway to a crawl space. Brushing away the cobwebs, Chase was able to locate the handle, and began to turn.

As the small door creaked open, the sounds became more pronounced. Chase got down on his hands and knees and crawled into the space. Taking out his flashlight, he was able to make his way down what appeared to be a narrow hallway, only to come across a set of circular stairs leading downward. This was unbelievable. It appeared to be some sort of secret passageway.

Still feeling as if something was moving him along, Chase tossed away any bit of remaining common sense and continued on.

At the bottom of the stairs, Chase came across what appeared to be another cellar-like space, but this time, he saw something he hadn't seen in the cellar above him: light. It appeared to be emanating from a nearby doorway. As he approached, he became aware that the smell of smoke was filling his nostrils. And while he should have taken this as his last and final clue to leave, he did what he thought any good reporter would do – he pressed on.

Turning the handle of the door, Chase entered the room, only to feel a dull thump on the head. Then came the blackness.

****

When he came to, Chase thought the room had somehow turned on its side. He then realized he was lying down. As he went to move, the reporter was met by a cruel surprise – his arms and legs had been tied down, rendering him immobile. The cool breeze told him his clothes had been stripped off as well. As Chase lay there naked and vulnerable, he was able to make out a dark shape from the corner of his eye. The shape seemed to be growing in size, although Chase realized the figure was just getting closer. As the shape entered within earshot, Chase screamed to be let go, but to no avail. His head hurt from what was obviously a deliberate blow, and the screaming only seemed to worsen his condition.

As the shape made his way around the table on which Chase was perched, a stunning revelation was uncovered: it was Julian Todd, the crooked local mayor.

Chase was shocked; he knew this guy was dirty, but this was beyond dirty.

"It's not going to do you any good to scream. No one can hear you down here."

The mayor seemed like a different person; there was evil in his eyes.

"Look, Julian, uh, Mr. Mayor. I don't know what you're

planning on doing, but I'm a newspaper reporter. Nobody tries to ..."

"Hush now," was the only response that came from Julian Toddy's mouth.

And with that, Chase felt the prick of a needle poke his vein, and for the second time tonight, the blackness enveloped him.

****

This time when he awoke, Chase was aware of other voices in the room. But blurred vision, coupled with the fact that he was unable to move his fastened head from side to side, rendered his detection skills useless.

There appeared to be some type of chanting going on, but the words this reporter couldn't make out. Again he tried to scream, but this time found he had no voice. Whatever was pumped into his veins clearly rendered his vocal cords useless.

Finally the chanting stopped, and Chase felt a figure approach. It was Julian Todd.

"Mr. Branson, why couldn't you just leave well enough alone. You see, this home is very important to my family, so of course I wanted to save it from near certain death." Although his mind was blurry, everything actually seemed to be getting quite clear as far as this old place was concerned. Chase thought the mayor and his cronies were the ones trying to stave off the house's slated demolition, and now he knew what his gut had told him was right. The only difference now is that he wasn't in much of a predicament to do anything about it.

"You see, my young friend, this house has been in my family for many years. That's right, I, Julian Todd Bell, am the rightful heir to this beautiful place."

Chase's heart skipped a beat: Bell. That was the name of the father and husband who the reporter read about in old news accounts. The man who went crazy and was sent to live out the remainder of his life in some mental hospital. The very man whose wife and children were never to be heard from again after his institutional commitment. The story was still fresh in Chase's mind.

The smile on Julian Todd's face told Chase the mayor knew exactly what the young reporter was thinking – that he had put two and two together.

"Well, it looks like your investigative skills finally got the better of you my young friend."

Chase wanted to ask Julian Todd why he was doing this, why he wanted to save the house so bad. And just why did he hide his link to the Bell family? Was he ashamed of what happened those many years ago.

"I can see you have questions, Chase. Too bad you can't ask them. But being the swell guy that I am, I'll go ahead and try to guess what it is that eats away at you. I'm guessing you want to know what this is supposed to be – the chanting, the rituals, you affixed to a table. Well, young man, I suppose I should tell you. After all, who are you going to repeat it to?

Chase, Thomas Bell was my great-grandfather. He moved his family here from Ireland when times were tough. He thought relocating to America would bring his loved ones some good fortune. But as he soon found out, there was nothing awaiting him except hardship and bad luck.

Thomas Bell was a man who wanted a better life for his family, but was instead met with the cold reality that a new country doesn't necessarily mean a fresh start."

Chase shot a look that said, 'what are you trying to say you lunatic, come out with it already,' but he couldn't very well formulate the thought into words, so he just continued to listen.

"You see, Chase, Thomas Bell was a man who reached wits end, and one night, while down in the wine cellar, he stumbled across the door in the back of the stairs. Feeling like he needed to retreat somewhere, other than to the bottom of a Whiskey bottle, my great-grandfather ventured to the lower level, but what he found would make him wish he never left the old country in the first place.

Half drunk and at the end of his rope, Thomas Bell began exploring the secret cellar, all the while cursing the world in general, praying there would be a way to put an end to his misery. Well, as they say young, curious reporter, be careful what you wish for. You see, Thomas Bell was praying, but it wasn't God that came calling, at least no God Mr. Thomas Bell was familiar with.

The whiskey must have gotten the better of him, because when Thomas Bell came to, he thought the whole thing was a dream, but it was much more real than that. The only thing he could remember as he made his way back upstairs was speaking to a blurry figure, one that said he would make everything better, if only Thomas Bell gave him three things. The old farmer agreed, although he wasn't able to remember what he offered up to satisfy the requests. Nevertheless, Thomas Bell began to write the whole thing off as a dream, that is until he reached the top floor. As he made his way to his kids' room, to say goodnight as had become his custom, he was horrified at what he came across. Inside his two children's beds were indeed his children, but not as he had left them. Their bodies were mangled and contorted beyond recognition. Their heads were twisted completely around, their eyes hung from their sockets and the blood, my God. It was everywhere.

Thomas Bell couldn't even scream. He was in total shock. Finally able to control himself, he made his way to his own bedroom to search out his wife, only to discover his spouse in much the same condition.

They were all dead, and Thomas Bell didn't know where to turn. What had happened here? He hadn't been away long. He was only downstairs – surely he would have heard something. Had someone broken into his house and murdered his loved ones in the cruelest of ways while he was passed out? The only thing he knew now is he needed help, so he immediately contacted the police."

Chase was frightened beyond belief, especially when confronting the fact that he was in a very precarious predicament in the very same cellar space he was now being told old Thomas Bell was in before learning of his family's horrible fate. He had to do something. But then he

185

told himself the sooner he confronted reality, the better off he'd be. He wasn't going anywhere, not at this stage in the game.

"Chase, are you still with me buddy?" Julian Todd asked, adopting a rather belittling tone. "Good, because I want you to hear this. After all, you're the curious reporter. Who else would be better equipped with this knowledge?

As I was saying, my great-grandfather told the cops what happened to his family, but when the authorities followed him back to the house, they found nothing like Thomas Bell described. You see, Chase, when they all got back to the house, they were greeted ... by Mrs. Bell and her two children. As would come as no surprise, Thomas Bell went beside himself at seeing what should have been his three dead family members in the flesh, welcoming police into their home as if nothing ever happened. This is when old Thomas Bell snapped. His mind was clearly gone, and when he tried to grab his shotgun, and blow away his loved ones ... well, let's just say that was the beginning of the end

186

for Mr. Thomas Bell.

You see, Chase, while my great-grandfather was in the midst of his maddening fit, he accused his 'returned' family members of having some sort of alignment with the Devil, thus leading to his decision to try and exterminate them. Little did he know how right he was."

Chase couldn't believe what he was hearing. This couldn't be true ...

"Oh, it's true," continued Julian Todd, responding as if he could read the reporter's mind. "Chase, I want you to listen very carefully. My great-grandfather had his prayers answered, his mind just couldn't handle what he had done. To put it in a way you can understand, young man, there are other gods out there besides yours, and Mr. Thomas Bell agreed to give away the souls of his loved ones in exchange for greater fortune. But he blocked the transaction out of his near-constant drunken mind for fear that what he had done would haunt him for the rest of his life. Well, that's exactly what happened. Basically, he lived out the rest of his days in a psychiatric ward, never

knowing who, or what, took the form of his wife and

children that night. He knew what he had seen, he knew

they were dead, but to the police, they were as real as you

and I. To the police, Mr. Thomas Bell was the one who was

off his rocker, and when he tried to shoot his family in front

of the officers ... well, that was the end of the road for my

great-grandfather."

****

The effects of whatever it was Julian Todd administered to

Chase were beginning to take their toll on the young

reporter. Oh how he wished he had left this story

untouched. But the dire situation told him it was too late

now; he had to live with his decisions – unfortunately,

living was not in his future.

"Chase, my family has been given the task of ensuring this

home remains standing. That was part of the deal, you see.

In exchange for my great-grandfather's deal with, well,

who he is isn't important. We were given the task of giving

188

our friend what he wants ... and what he wants are human souls. But we don't like people to interfere with our duties. That poor family that moved in here 10 years ago ... should never have happened. However they came to be the home's owners, and I still don't know how that one slipped through, that just didn't matter in the end. My father made sure they regretted the day they ever set foot on our property. Right dad?"

Chase could see that Julian Todd turned his head to another spot in the room. "That's right son," came the response. Something wasn't right; Chase knew that voice. As his mind was searching for the origin of the voice, he was spared any more guessing when the figure approached.

"So, we meet again my young friend."

Chase couldn't believe his eyes. Standing before him was his friend, Tobin Mansfield, the old man who he had grown close with since becoming a reporter.

Chase was finally able to muster up enough strength to utter two words: "Mr. Mansfield," he said in a soft, strained voice.

"I thought I told you to call me Tobin," came the shrewd reply. "Well, since you can't seem to remember that, I'll lay a new one on you – please, call me by my birth name, John Bell.

****

The last thoughts to go through Chase Branson's mind were mundane ones, like the fact that he never should have chosen journalism as a profession, or at least that he never should have let one story get the better of him. But none of that mattered. At this point, although he was never the religious type, Chase Branson opted to make his peace with his own God, and let nature take its course. Unfortunately for him, this end he would not wish on his worst enemies. As he lay there, awaiting the torture that would surely accompany the reignited chanting, Chase Branson could only think Julian Todd had somewhat of a soft spot for him, even though the mayor clearly saw the young reporter as a threat. After all, why else would Julian Todd dope him up?

But before he could finish asking the question to himself,

Chase Branson noticed the numbing agent wearing off. So

much for wishful thinking. Besides, he should have known

better – wishful thinking is what landed this otherwise

promising reporter in this position in the first place.

Curiosity and desire are bad, folks. One lesson Chase

Branson learned that the hard way.

Jon Campisi has been a fan of all things horror for as long as he can remember.

His affinity for the dark, depraved and horrific is starkly contrasted with his friendly, sweet and welcoming demeanor.

A Keystone State native who has lived most of his life in southeastern Pennsylvania, Jon is a versatile scribe, having dabbled in both fiction and nonfiction.

He spent a good part of his professional career in journalism.

These days, when not penning horrific tales, Jon works as the director of communications for his family's financial planning firm.

He is also a freelance reporter and amateur photographer.

Jon resides in Philadelphia with his wife and two dogs.